A sensuous, passionate story of first love, first baby, *The Best Thing* captures brilliantly the turmoil in Melanie's life and the intensity of her pleasures and pains. Margo Lanagan uses words as though they were new minted— as though she were inside the skin of a teenager. But there is more to the novel than that. In a natural, unforced way it shows Mel's growing understanding of love, individuality and responsibility.

This is a thought-provoking, life-affirming book— and a great read.

MARGO LANAGAN was born in 1960 and has lived in Sydney, Melbourne, London, Perth, Mundrabilla and Paris. She studied history at the University of Sydney. She works as a writer and book editor, and lives with her partner and their two sons in Sydney's inner west.

Her writing includes novels for teenagers and adults—*The Best Thing* and *Touching Earth Lightly*—and for younger readers—*Wildgame, The Tankermen* and *Walking Through Albert.*

MARGO LANAGAN

THE best THING

 **ark** fiction

ALLEN & UNWIN

The writing of this book was assisted by the Commonwealth Government through the Australia Council, its arts funding and advisory body.

Australia Council
for the Arts

A Little Ark Book
First published in 1995 by
Allen & Unwin
9 Atchison Street
St Leonards NSW 1590
Australia

Phone: (61 2) 8425 0100
Fax: (61 2) 9906 2218
E-mail: frontdesk@allen-unwin.com.au
Web: http://www.allen-unwin.com.au

National Library of Australia
Cataloguing-in-Publication entry:
Lanagan, Margo.
The best thing.
ISBN 1 86448 824 7.
1. Title.
A823.3

Set in New Baskerville
Cover designed by Ruth Grüner
Text designed by Rosanna Di Risio
Cover photograph by Thomas Schweizer
Printed in Australia by McPherson's Printing Group, Victoria

3 5 7 9 10 8 6 4

ACKNOWLEDGEMENTS

Muhammad Ali's words on page 7 are from his autobiography, *I Am the Greatest*. The definitions of 'pug' on page 14 are from the *New Shorter Oxford English Dictionary*, Oxford University Press, 1993 edition. The paragraphs on life before birth on pages 24, 27, 39, 43–4, 51–2, 53 and 77–8 owe a great deal to two articles in *Life* magazine: 'Drama of Life Before Birth', 30 April 1965 and 'The First Days of Creation', August 1990. Any errors arising from their paraphrasing are the author's responsibility. The quotations on pages 54, 97 and 113 are taken from the Right Honourable Dame Edith Summerskill, *The Ignoble Art*, published by William Heinemann in 1956. Muhammad Ali's words on page 87 are quoted in the introduction to Peter Heller (ed.), *In this Corner! 40 World Champions Tell Their Stories*, Simon & Schuster, New York, 1973. The quotations on pages 92 and 105–6 are from National Health and Medical Research Council, *Health Aspects of Boxing*, AGPS, Canberra, 1975. The scoring guidelines on page 99 are from the Australian Boxing Association, *Referees' and Judges' Manual*, 10th edition, 1962. The neurologist's words on page 101 were cited in an article by Peter Fitzsimons published in the *Sydney Morning Herald* on 14 February 1990, 'The hazy zone was unknown to Tyson'. The quotation on page 124 is from an article by Peter Fitzsimons and Daniel Williams in the *Sydney Morning Herald* on 20 March 1990, and is used with permission. Kostya Tszyu's words on page 127 are taken from an interview by Alan Attwood, 'Eyes on the Prize', published in the *Sydney Morning Herald* on 12 November 1994, and are used with permission. Jeff Fenech's words about Johnny Lewis on pages 133-4 are from an article by Peter Muszkat, 'Lord of the Ring', published in *The Australian Magazine* on 23 September 1989, and are used with permission. The quotation on page 140 is from Peter Corris's history of Australian boxing, *Lords of the Ring*, Cassell Australia, 1980, and is used with permission. The quotation on page 159 is from Casey Meyers, *Walking: A Complete Guide to the Complete Exercise*, Random House, New York, © Casey Meyers 1992, and is used with permission. The quotation on page 169 is from Deirdre Bair, *Simone de Beauvoir: A Biography*, Vintage Books, London, © Deirdre Bair 1990.

Every effort has been made to obtain permission to use these quotations. The author welcomes contact from publishers to rectify any errors or omissions.

1

HALF-DREAM ROOM

The feeling is like being half awake and half dreaming . . . And your awake half knows what you're dreaming about. A heavy blow takes you to the door of this room. It opens and you see neon, orange and green lights blinking. You see bats blowing trumpets, alligators play trombones, and snakes are screaming. Weird masks and actors' clothes hang on the wall.

Muhammad Ali

I find a condom in my locker, with a jelly baby poked right down to the tip. The baby's had to be flattened to fit through the locker slots. I glimpse its squashed round face as I gather it up in a tissue, find myself tracing its life history, back into the box with its fellow babies, up into the machine that counts jelly babies into boxes, up along the conveyor belt through the drier, to the nozzles that squirt the exact amounts of jelly goop into the baby moulds. Gloved, hair-netted, white-coated workers in attendance: mould scrubbers, defect spotters, nozzle cleaners. These thoughts get me through the crush, out of the building, through the gate.

Brenner comes up to me—no, he comes *after* me. Wants to know why we 'broke up'. Why we can't be friends.

'Oh, you tell *me*,' I say, not even stopping.

'Why?' he says, all innocent. 'We didn't have a fight or anything, did we?'

'No, we didn't. You just disappeared off the face of the earth at the first stupid rumour, that's all.' I stride on, trying to get ahead of him.

'What rumour?'

I snort.

'Honest, I didn't hear anything!'

'Bullshit you didn't.'

He jogs up the path behind me. 'Okay, so I did hear rumours. But there was nothing to 'em. I didn't *believe* 'em or anything.'

'You're talking too much. Go away and leave me alone.'

He walks along beside me to the crossing, expecting me to wait there. I go straight across the street, forcing cars to stop for me.

'Hey, wait on!'

'What's the matter, Bren?' I say over my shoulder. 'Suddenly you're all matey again. I don't want you coming home with me, so you'd better tell me quick what's on your mind.'

'I dunno. I just saw Lisa today, and, gee, she's being such a ratbag about you. Like, she was your best friend, wasn't she?'

'What, you feel sorry for me, do you? Well, wow, so I suppose I should feel flattered. What is it, three months now? A quarter of a year? I appreciate your concern, Bren, I really do.' My throat is starting to close over, and I have to walk on.

'Mel, don't be like this.' He's following me again.

Like this! I turn on him, way past anger. 'Hey, Brenner, I think it's really, really big of you to come round to my side of things after dropping me like a hot potato, for no reason, without even discussing it, three months ago.'

'Come on, Mel, I didn't know who to believe!'

'How about *me*?' Our faces are only centimetres apart before he backs up a bit. I go on yelling. 'What was wrong with coming to me, for my side of the story? I was the girlfriend, I was the one you were supposed to be able to talk to about *anything*.'

Brenner's eyes are all over the place looking for a way out. He's pathetic. 'Well, I felt uncomfortable, you know? The things people were saying about you—'

'Like what?'

'Well, Lisa said you were—' He looks at me and his eyes have got a horrible expression in them. He's really curious, greedy to know. 'That you were pregnant, and everything.'

'What do you mean, *and everything*? What else?'

'She said you hadn't told her who, but that she figured it couldn't have been me, from what you said.'

'"She said, she figured." You two've been having a good old chat, haven't you?'

He's not pretending to want to be friends any more. He's just busting to know. 'Well?' he says. He's practically twitching, practically on his tippy-toes.

I almost start to enjoy myself. 'Well what?'

'How much of it's true?'

I look him up and down, very slowly. It's not as if he even cares. Not about me, not about what happened. He's just digging for gossip, hunting for stuff to shout at me tomorrow, when I walk past him and his mates at the school gate.

I shake my head. 'It's too late for you to expect an answer to that.'

'What?' He puts his hands on his hips. Oh, he's just *so tired* of dealing with idiots like me.

'Three months ago you might have got a straight answer. But after all that carrying on during the exams last year, and pretending I didn't exist over Christmas—no *way*. And all this shit you've been giving me since school got back—God, what Lisa's doing is nothing!' It's not true, but it sounds good. 'You can get stuffed. I don't need you around. I don't need shits like you.'

He grabs my shoulder. I slap his hand away and back off.

'It's true, isn't it?' His face turns ugly. I start to put distance between us. He shouts across it, 'You *were* up the duff to some bloke, like they all reckon!'

They all. *They all*. Who? How many? I concentrate on keeping my head up, my steps steady.

'You *did* have an abortion! You're just a *slut*! You were sleeping with this guy all the time, weren't you!' I can't see why he's not following me, hitting me. I try to walk faster without seeming to. 'It's no wonder no-one talks to you. No-one likes a *slut*!' He loves saying that word. He loves being angry, being so *right*, and swearing at me. Words of Power, that's what Mum calls swearwords. I call out over my shoulder, 'Sticks and stones, Brenner.'

My voice is too high, but he's not listening. A dog behind a tin fence starts yapping like a maniac.

A stone whacks my schoolbag, another hits my leg. The Words of Power beat on my back. I feel as if there's a whole posse of schoolmates and parents behind me; Brenner's their mouthpiece, no more than that, just the noisiest, angriest one in the pack. 'Fucking bitch! You'd sleep with anyone! Do you do it with *animals* too? With *dogs*?'

So I think of Pug. Sometimes he wears a crazy-about-me expression that for a second makes me feel like a good person, a nice person. Then Brenner is just a mistake anyone might make, Lisa a nobody. Sometimes Pug says, in a really *doleful* voice, 'You're so *smart*, you know? You're too smart for me, I reckon.'

Brenner isn't following any more. I refuse to look round, but he sounds distant, incoherent. Stones whizz in the air, but I'm getting out of range.

He's scared to ask for the truth, to ask properly, one person to another. They all are. You give them the truth and they don't know what to do with it except use it against you.

Cars stop for me at the Salisbury Road crossing, and I almost cry with gratitude. It feels as if the drivers are being incredibly kind to me, as if they know my leg and head are stinging from the stones and my knees are wobbling, and they're stopping to help me escape, and maybe block the way if Brenner comes after me again.

I make it home without having a major heart attack. Mum's in the garden on a flex day, gouging weeds out of our tiny front lawn.

'Hi,' I say.

'Oh, hullo,' she says, smiling up at me. 'Just taking out my executive stress on a few dandelions.' This is a joke—she's got one of those public-service jobs where her title is longer than her working day. 'You look hot.'

'Yes.' All my injuries are out of her sight. Blood weaves through

12

the hair on the back of my head. 'I'll change and get us a drink, hey?'

Up in the bathroom's coolness, I shower and rinse my hair, press my finger to the cut to stop the bleeding, put on clean clothes. I can almost forget it's Tuesday, almost not care about tomorrow. *Bugger Brenner*, I can think. *And bugger Lisa and Donna and all the gossips at that bloody school.* I am not going to *let* them make my hands shake. I'm not going to *let* them make me sick with dread when I open my eyes to face another school day. They can *forget* it.

I can think these things, up here. Now.

I thought Brenner, for sure, was the sort of guy I was supposed to aim for. Good looking in a really wholesome, blond way. Sporty, cool. Muscle-headed. Insensitive. Shit-for-brains. If I put him next to Pug I can hardly believe they're the same species. The difference is so huge, just between the ways I feel about them. With Pug, I *feel for* him, whereas with Brenner I *thought about* him. I *observed* myself with him. I was always the watcher. I never really cared much. I was too busy being pleased I had someone. Any guy would have done, but having someone so good looking, someone everyone approved of, was a bonus. If he'd died (falling during a rock-climb, maybe, or being run over during a bike race) I could have got off on playing the tragedy queen for a while, but I don't think my life would have fallen apart.

Don't I sound cold? It was different when I was with him. It was a big ego-boost, and I was *in love* because every other girl I knew was in love with *someone*. So I floated around, too, I smiled at everyone, I kept a diary full of *movie ticket stubs*, of *pressed flowers*, of bits of *poems* Brenner would have curled up and died to read, some I wrote myself and some I pinched from books. (I burned it over Christmas, ceremonially, in the backyard, when Mum and Dad were out.) I drew our initials twined together in secret squiggly parts of drawings I did in Art at school, and pointed them out to Lisa. I remember she squealed in rapture and immediately started working on a monogram for her and James, which was out of date by the time those pieces got marked; she was with Terry by then. Oh God, I did all sorts of stuff because it was the thing to do. I thought I meant some of it, but most of it was a big act, a waste of time.

And then life gets *serious*, and you look back and realise what a *kid* you were, playing at being grown up.

pug /pʌg/ *n.*[5] *slang*. M19 [Abbrev.] = PUGILIST

But for **pug** *n.*[2], other meanings:

> A term of endearment: dear one.
> A courtesan, a prostitute; a mistress.
> A monkey, an ape. Also (*rare*), a child.
> A small demon or imp; a sprite.
> (*pug-dog*) A dwarf breed of dog resembling a bulldog, with a broad flat nose and a deeply wrinkled face.
> A short or stumpy person or thing; *esp.* a dwarf.
> (*pug-engine*) A small locomotive used chiefly for shunting purposes.

For **pug** *v.*[1] *t.*:

> Dirty by excessive handling.[!]

For **pug** *v.*[2] *t.*:

> Thrust, poke or pack into a space . . . Prepare (clay for brickmaking or pottery, by kneading and working into a soft and plastic condition).

Thursday night at the supermarket. Cruel place: fluorescent lights (too many), metal shelving, shiny trolleys snarling and queuing, frazzled families, and over all the racket 'Franklins' Radio' smarming on, alerting you to bargains in the meat department, the dairy, wherever, calling you 'shoppers' as if you had no other function in life. Too much stock, too many colours and shiny packets; it wears out your eyes.

I report back to Mum with the butter and yoghurt. 'How come Dad doesn't come with us any more? We used to get this done in half the time.'

'Would you come, if you could avoid it?' Mum watches somebody's three-year-old tear open a packet of Smarties and send half of them skittering across the floor.

'We used to have fun, I thought.' She gives me an ironic look. 'I mean, I don't mean we *don't* have fun now.'

'Of course not.' Mum sighs and runs her thumb down her list.

'I *do-on't*! Just—it used to be a quick shop and then a big long treat, like going out to dinner. Now it's spending forever in here and then grabbing an ice-cream on the way out. Bor-ring.'

'We can eat here if you like, downstairs. We'll get the frozen stuff on the way out—no, forget I said that. I couldn't stand another dose of supermarket queues. We can do something, though. Oh, look! There's your mate Lisa.'

'Quick! What d'you want me to get? I don't want her to see me!'

'Why ever not?'

'We're having a fight! What do you want, *quick*!'

'Orange juice. And apple. Morningtown!' She calls out after me. 'Not that reconstituted stuff!'

The shopping turns into a nightmare of dodging around shelves and trying to keep track of where Lisa is. But at the checkout, as if fate drove us together, her dad calls out, 'Well, if it ain't the Dows! Having a night out on the town, are we, ladies?' He manoeuvres his trolley in behind ours.

Mum jokes back, and I smile weakly. My eyes drag themselves to Lisa. Even in this spotlight-every-zit lighting she looks flawless. She's all Sixtied up, in a white mini-dress with a chain belt, white sandals with daisies on them, clanking bangles. Her lips shimmer pale in her golden face and her eyes are made up to look huge and luminous. When she sees me, though, she forgets the waif look she's trying for. She goggles at me, her pink-iced lips pressed together; then she lets her gaze wander away over the checkouts, a superior smile on her face.

Pug's room is always a pigsty. Dead socks, dead magazines, the bed always unmade. There's a smell. I guess part of it must be dead-sock smell. Another part is the frangipani tree at the window, its flower-stars' sweetness complicating the light. Also dust, and the sheets, of course. Sheets, even fresh from the laundrette, can only take so much wear and tear, so much steaming and soaking and drying and being lain on. They start to live, to have their own breath. I couldn't name for you what his scent is *like*; it's not like any of its parts. I step in here and breathe it, and it's relief, it's excitement. It's Pug's own territory. Nobody comes here but us.

We are *ages* in that queue—so long I think I'm going to faint with the tension and the processed air. Finally we get out, Mum waving Mr Wilkinson a cheery goodbye. 'Boy, you really are having a fight, aren't you?' she murmurs as I hurry her down the ramp. 'What's it all about?'

'Her being a *shitbag*.' I feel sick. I feel as if I'll never be free of Lisa, never get out from under her mushroom-cloud of influence.

'Ah.' Mum nods wisely. 'So is our junk-food tea still on, or do you want to get as far away from Lisa as possible?'

'Let's go home,' I say. 'Maybe Dad'll take us out for tea anyway.'

'He'll be *too tired*.' She imitates the way Dad slumps when he says that. 'He's always too tired these days to do anything with his *family*. Old age is creeping up on him, poor bloke.'

'He's working pretty hard, though.'

'Yeah. For some reason.'

I grin at her. 'Like, maybe he wants to earn squillions?'

'Well, I'm still waiting for all this extra effort to show up on the bank statements; that's all I can say.'

In the rooftop carpark a pearly-pink sunset (about the same shade as Lisa's lipstick) lights up the rows of car roofs. Shunting cars fart into the sea-touched breeze. I breathe the whole cocktail gratefully; there *is* life after Franklins.

Ricky Lewis, old friend of Mum's and Dad's, is there when we get home.

''Day, Rick,' says Mum. 'Why aren't *you* out Thursday-night shopping?' We struggle through the loungeroom with our grocery bags.

'I'm having it delivered these days. It's fabulous. I told you about this guy. I tick off what I want and he puts it on my doorstep next day.'

'Oh, but you're missing a marvellous cultural experience, isn't she, Mel?' Mum dumps her bags on the kitchen table. Dad's in there getting glasses out of the cupboard. He looks as if he's been caught in a blizzard: hair every which way, tie loose, collar unbuttoned. 'You should come with us next week, like old times,' Mum says to him.

'Yeah, I should,' he says, more enthusiastically than you'd expect. Mum and I make surprised faces at each other. 'You do *want* a beer, don't you, Ricky?' he calls out. 'You didn't actually answer me before these people came barging in.'

She comes to the kitchen door, leans there. 'Don't mind if I do.' She's wearing quite short shorts and a T-shirt that's tight enough to show off her breasts. The nipples stand out under the cloth—it's pretty hard not to notice them. How embarrassing. Why can't she fold her arms, instead of tucking her hands in the back of her waistband like that?

'And for the workers?' Dad's at the fridge, getting out a beer-bottle. He sees me looking at him and smiles a funny smile, bright and self-conscious, with the eyebrows going.

'No thanks,' I say. 'Nothing for me.'

We never pull the bedclothes over ourselves. I often wonder what'd happen if Mum and Dad burst in on us. What I'd do—I wouldn't scream or sit up or anything dumb—I'd lie there just as I was, my head on his shoulder, my arm around his chest. He'd tense up, but I'd say, 'It's okay,' and we'd both just go on staring at the ceiling, breathing slowly, while Dad shouted and Mum went white in the doorway.

His hands are big, strong, really *male*. (I put my hand against Pug's and it's a slip of a hand, meant for different operations from his. And I'm a slip of a girl, up against him.) His arm is heavy on my chest and stomach, and the fingers rest as a cage around my breast.

Sometimes we lie like that for *hours*. And then one of us wakes up and starts exploring, and then the other, and then before you know it . . . well, words are hopeless to describe it when it's good, and it's always good. I keep on expecting annoyance, that *besieged* feeling I got with Brenner, but it hasn't happened yet.

Scene: Kitchen, last October. MUM is putting away shopping.
 ME enters.

ME: Mum, I've missed two periods.

(MUM freezes. Long silence.)

MUM *(turning to face ME)*: Does this mean what I think it
 means?

ME: I think so.

(Long silence.)

MUM: Brenner?

(ME nods.)

MUM *(chirpy, bitter)*: Well, at least you know *that*. *(Long silence.)*
 Have you decided what you'll do?

ME *(gigantically grateful that she's not screaming/crying/fainting)*:
 No.

MUM *(tentatively)*: Keep? *(After a pause, with a catch in her voice)*
 Get rid of?

ME *(ironically)*: Like, kill?

MUM *(shrugging)*: It's an option. These days, in this country.
 An option and an age-old practice, there's no getting
 away from it. I mustn't talk. *(Shakes herself.)* I mustn't be
 seen to . . .

ME *(bitterly)*: . . . to care one way or the other.

MUM: Oh, sweetheart, *care*! *(Crosses room, puts arms around ME. ME starts crying. Softly)*: Oh, God. My baby girl. For crying out loud! Darling, darling . . . *(Sits ME down, pulls chair to face me.)* I know you must be in a mess, hovering, but I can't make a decision for you. I mustn't pressure you one way or another. Which way are you leaning, Mel? Towards Keep or Get Rid Of?

ME *(through sobs)*: Get—Get Rid Of. It's too big. And scary.

MUM: All right, then. Let me think. Let me think.

Pug tells me I'm beautiful. 'Beaudifuw' is how he says it. 'Your face—I dunno, you look like . . . like a princess or sumpthink.' *A princess or sumpthink.* I love him. I love it how he looks at me as if I *am* a princess (or sumpthink), way up out of reach, and he's a foot soldier or a stablehand or some lowly crumb on the footpath, just *adoring* me. Does Dad ever look at Mum like that, completely adoring, completely lost in her? *Did* he ever? Maybe once he did. Things *must* have been better once, before they got bogged down in the suburbs, trekking back and forth to offices, wiping crumbs off kitchen benches, mending broken bloody *light fittings*, for God's sake! The idea of them spending time together for the sheer pleasure of being together . . . sorry, guys, me no compute. Maybe they don't compute either, any more. Funny how little a person can know about her parents, even after sixteen years and seven months in the same house.

Pug looks tall to me, me being short. He looks solid, me being skinny. He looks dark-skinned because I am pale.

He's stronger than Brenner would ever've dreamed of trying to be, from all the training. The sit-ups make his belly hard, hard as bone, the muscles banded like extra ribs. I've nearly passed out being hugged by this guy; the blood stops in my head, blackness fogs my eyes, twinkles away when he lets go. And then he's looking down on me, through squiggling stars. The cleanest eyes, green-grey, with white whites. In a movie once, a boy took a pickaxe to the eyes of a stableful of horses. Looking in Pug's eyes, I feel like saying, *Watch out for that boy, watch out for that pickaxe.* They're so fitted and framed, so shiny in the gloom, it's as if he's presenting them for injury. His mouth is the same in its softness, its definite line asking to be blurred or broken. The skin on him! I can feel it on my lips now, under my fingers. It just seems to flow with energy. And he's always so warm; it's almost like a breeze of warm atoms coming off him—I can feel it on my face when he's close.

It's a relief sometimes to get out and see old or ugly faces in King Street, faces on which the blows have already fallen, that wrinkle and sag and look tired. There isn't that tension in my chest, then, of waiting, of having to keep watch.

Of course, it works the other way, coming from that plain old ugly injured world to this: smooth-carved skin, animal-warm, asking to be touched. It's easier for my eyes and hands, harder for my heart.

The gym is perhaps three times the size of Pug's bedroom. Sometimes there are twenty people in there: six or seven working out, the two trainers, and others resting, along the walls or the bench by the ring. There's a window, very small, very high up, almost apologising for having to let in some light. Nobody says much, only Jimmy the trainer, moving around the ring with punching pads on his hands, chanting sequences of blows to the boy he's working.

You feel as if your brain's being pummelled, the punishment those pads, the bag, the punchball, the air are taking. It's crowded just with real people, and then there are all the imaginary opponents, dodging, throwing curly ones, copping body blows. Sometimes it gets so busy I forget it's Pug I'm here with. And then he's there beside me on the bench, breathing hard, elbows on knees, T-shirt wet-rippled like beach sand up his back. His guard is

20

up—a carefully immobile face, looking past me if he talks to me, not smiling. I might get a flicker of him now and then, but mostly I have to wait until later, when we go back to his place.

Everyone wears the same slack, preoccupied expression. Everyone bar Jimmy and his assistant is running sweat. It has no smell, as if these bodies are rinsed of all toxins and stream pure water. Morning and evening the floorboards are soaked with it, like a ritual; it's steamed and flung into the air; one boy always spits in the ring, and rubs it into the general sog with the toe of his training shoe; once I was watching Pug spar with Justin Silva and a drop hit me right in the eye. Bodies are like big wet fruit; they thwack and smack and squelch when they collide, and the juice flies out of them.

I tell him about my bad day yesterday. 'This guy I used to go out with was hassling me,' is how I put it.

'He wants you back, does he?' says my Pug, very serious.

'He hates my guts. He chucked stones at me.' I show him the mark on my leg, the scab in my hair. I start to feel bad about this, like a sook, trying to get sympathy.

Well, I get it. He goes very quiet, won't look at me. Then he *does* look, and his heart's going so hard that his head is shaking, and his hands shake too, and I feel like a complete arsehole for having said anything.

'I could kill that bloke,' he says. 'And if *you* told me to, I reckon I'd do it.' The way he says 'you', grabbing my arms, peering in through one of my eyes, then the other—my guts feel like concrete with the guilt. I did *ask* for all that shit from Brenner, after all.

I close my eyes and kiss him. He kisses me back very fiercely, and ⊕⊖. It's excellent. The anger and the . . . well, I guess the guilt helps. I really get lost there for a little while, really forget about my life and the mess it's turning into.

After, he wants to talk more about Brenner, but I won't. I joke him out of it. I don't want to go into all that stuff with Pug. This is completely different, what I've got with him, completely separate. I wanted it to stay like that—what a dickhead for even mentioning it!

But I had the bad taste of it in my mouth, and he's the only one. Now my mouth is full of the taste of his, and my nose full of the salty-olive smell of him, and my . . . yes, *I* am full of the feeling of him, which isn't just, like, a plug and a socket fitting together, but ripples all round my body, and my . . . whatever it is, whatever else there is.

The question of meeting the family. 'Oh, man, does this mean we're engaged?' I joke.

'I just wanna show you off,' says Pug, grinning. 'And I think you and my mum'd get on okay.'

'Oh God, but what about the other three?'

'Yeah, they'd be cool.'

'Going on previous experience . . .?'

'There *isn't* any previous experience.' My words sound very much *mine* coming out of his mouth. 'That's why they'd be cool.'

'Amazed, eh? Do they think you're gay or something?'

He emerges from the shadow at the bedhead. His eyes hold the window-light in their greenness, in their curved lenses. 'You're trying to wriggle out of this, aren't you?'

I cave in, nodding. He looks at me harder until I turn away.

'Are you really scared?'

'Yeah. I am.' I shrug off the urge to cry.

'Why, but?' He's right up close and unavoidable. 'They're just *people*.'

'They're *your* people. And anyway . . . I'm not all that good with people.'

'Me-el!' He flops back on the bed, then straight away sits up at me again. 'What are you, some kind of bloody *extra-terrestrial* or something?'

'Gee, that's a big word,' I snap, so quick and sour we gape at each other. Then Pug cracks up, and I have to too.

22

When we emerge from it, he grips my shoulders. 'You are so stupid ('sjupid' is how he says it). How could anyone not like you?'

'Oh, look, it beats me.' I smile straight into his face.

He's lying behind me. He speaks into my neck. 'Jimmy said again I could go professional.'

'Oh?'

'Yeah. Anytime I want, he reckons.'

'And do you want?'

He laughs unhappily. 'Can't think of anything else to do with myself. You know, I could say I've got a job, then.'

'You'd lose the dole?'

'I'd make okay money. I mean, I do all right on the dole, but it'd be good not to be on it, for a change. They'd stop hassling me about bloody training schemes and résumé writing and shit. *Office procedures*, they want me to get skilled in next. Christ.'

'So you'll probably do it.'

'Probably, yeah.' He lies thinking. 'Yeah, you're right—I have decided, really.'

'Oh, well.' As if I'm saying goodbye. As if he's walking away down some tunnel I'm not allowed to enter. 'Try not to get knocked out too often, hey? I've heard it's really bad for your brain.'

He clears the hair from my neck, kisses me there. 'Does fuck-all for the ego, too. So I've heard. I've been lucky so far, anyway.'

'Well, if anyone deserves to have their luck hold . . .'

'Yeah, like, I haven't got much brains to spare, hey.'

'That's not what I *meant*.' I'm savage with it, savage with finding I care.

Whenever I walk home from there I feel so good about myself—confident and beautiful. He makes me that way. I go there to be polished and brushed until I shine, and I walk back shining. It

23

doesn't matter that I'm in my 'invisible uniform'—black jeans and T-shirt, hair falling around my face. It doesn't matter that people don't turn to look at me twice as I walk past. I *know* I'm shining. I'm shining *inside*.

I can't stop thinking about him—don't want to. 'I love him.' I only have to think the words, never mind all the memories that spill from them like marbles, and my heart lifts into a higher gear. And he loves me, the way he looks at me, and touches me really carefully as if he's scared I might push his hand away any moment. I can set my whole self, body and whatever-else-goes-with-it (these are the only times, actually, when I think maybe I might have a *soul*) practically singing, just thinking back, going from peak moment to peak moment. I sit in school, I lie awake in the dark at home, singing.

> Two hours: Ejected into her fallopian tube, a woman's egg, or ovum, will float there, fertile, for about twenty-four hours. Nutrient cells halo the hungry egg, and a crowd of sperm cells is busy tearing these nutrients from the ovum in preparation for drilling through the outer egg wall. A dozen sperm, rotating themselves into the wall with strong tail-beats, will be close to penetrating at the same time, but when the first one is through, the wall changes chemical composition to prevent the others piercing it. The successful sperm continues to drill through the inner wall, relinquishing its tail once this is accomplished.

Midnight. City glare hazes out the stars at my window, framed by twitching ivy. Another weird quiet night. It's not like Dad's a really noisy man, but when he's not here our house is different. Mum just makes a sort-of dinner, scrappy, not a proper meal, and then sits down and writes letters all evening, or goes and has a long bath. If I try to start a conversation she talks back as if she's not really here—or maybe as if *I'm* not really here. Since last year, whenever Dad's around we make a lot of cheerful noise, and whenever he's not here we're really quiet, as if we've exhausted ourselves. I don't know what Mum's thinking about, but I find my mind goes to work on things, from the darkness outside the house walls to the watch on my bedside table, so that they *lurk*, instead of just *being*. They watch. They brood on me. Sometimes I make myself so scared I can't move.

God, Dad, you don't do much these days except go to work and come home and sleep. What a life! How do you stand it? I thought he must be making stacks. I asked him if he was, wondering if he had a different house in mind, or some kind of fancy holiday like he used to talk about. But he said not many of the new clients were coming through. 'Makes it really worthwhile working late, then, hey,' I said. But he went on about goodwill, and building up trust with clients, and how he *didn't expect me to understand yet*, and that got me off the topic. I got mad at him instead. How old does he think I am, six instead of sixteen? I can't believe how *patronising* he was.

'Don't go slamming off to your room, Miss Sensitive!' he yelled after me as I ran upstairs, and I heard him going on to Mum. 'What's the matter with her these days? You can't say *anything* without her doing her block!' I lay on my bed thinking maybe I *had* overreacted, but certainly not feeling bad enough to go down and apologise.

Things with Dad are stuffed. He doesn't want to understand how things work in my life. I remember, trying to tell him about the way the HSC units work, when I was trying to plan Year 11, and he just pulled away, physically, even. Real distaste came onto his face and he found an excuse to be somewhere else fast. I know he didn't have a great time at school, but couldn't he take an interest? He doesn't have to do the work, just know what I'm doing and be encouraging. But every time the subject of school comes up he dips out. Sometimes he even says, 'Oh well, school was never my strong point. I left after Fourth Form to work on building sites'—and you can *still* see the relief on his face from twenty-five years ago! Seems like a long time to carry around a grudge.

It's not just that sort of thing. It's last year, and the way Mum and I coped with my little *crisis* with Brenner. Dad never knew a thing—it wasn't a family matter, it was a women's matter, and somehow that put Dad on the outer and he's never found his way back in.

And the stupid thing was, we didn't have to plan anything. Two days before I was booked in to get rid of it, the baby got rid of itself. I needn't even have told Mum. I could've just gone on like normal and there'd've been no disruption. I remember lying in bed after having been to the hospital, wishing and wishing I'd kept my mouth shut. Dad came in thinking it was just a bad period, patted my hot-water bottle, said some oh-well-better-in-the-morning thing, went out. I felt like such a fake, and I also couldn't work out what was going on, why he couldn't be told. 'He'd be upset,' Mum had said, but I didn't feel any better for having him *not* be upset. Nowadays I keep finding myself on the verge of telling him, just to clear things up, just to get him in from the outer, but I always chicken out. Mum was serious, quiet, almost fearful, and after Lisa I've learned to keep my mouth shut when in doubt.

Ah, here's Dad now. Phew, now the house feels normal. Up the stairs, past my door, into the bathroom, shower on. He must be the cleanest man on earth, showering morning and night. It's not like they'd get up to anything much dirty in the night, Mum fast asleep when he gets in.

Oh no, they're having a bit of a talk, Mum sounding dozy, Dad quiet. A little laugh (like, *little*—no happiness in it, nothing to get excited about).

A few minutes later: now I guess they've settled in to sleep. What must that be like, sleeping next to the same person for twenty years? Well, sleeping next to anyone at all, through the night. Couples in the movies, it's either burning passion or older people in pyjamas turning their backs on each other—no clues. With Brenner the idea never occurred to me. It was quick sex snatched anywhere half-private and no hanging around afterwards. I couldn't understand what all the fuss was about, certainly why *girls* were talking about it as if it were *so* important. I couldn't see what the *girl* got out of any of it. I wonder about spending a whole night with Pug, though. It might be nice. I know he'd like the idea; it'd only be up to me to suggest it. Maybe if we're still together next year, when I'm out of school and free . . . when life's had a chance to get good again. I sure don't want to add any complications now.

Ambra Lewis gives me a weird look. I just catch the end of it before she turns back to her friends. It's a really hard, watchful look, like she's just properly noticed me for the first time. Did you tell Ricky Lewis, Mum? She *is* probably your best mate, and you tell her practically every thought in your head. Well, maybe she's not such a great friend, if she's blabbed to Ambra.

Or maybe it's on the grapevine and everyone knows about it, from Lisa or Brenner or whoever'd be creepy enough to pass it on. Maybe the rumour just hit Year 10 and Ambra's in shock.

Or maybe she's always hated my guts and this is just the first time I've actually caught her showing it. Why should I care what Ambra Lewis thinks?! Stuff her!

After twenty hours, two small chromosome-filled bubbles float inside the egg, one provided by the woman and one by the man. They combine to form a single nucleus containing all the genetic information needed for the creation of a new individual human person. About twelve hours later the cell divides for the first time, into two. Division and growth will continue for nine months. The cell cluster begins its journey toward the uterus, propelled on waves made by hairlike cilia that line the fallopian tube. Despite all this activity, no biological signal tells her that fertilisation has occurred.

'Hey, you wanna come and sit with us, Mel?' I looked up and Lisa had me in her sights. But nobody around her was stifling giggles; nobody seemed particularly interested, even.

'Oh, okay.' It can't hurt, I thought. Little did I know.

Lisa can make you feel very interesting, all of a sudden. She can be super-friendly, and stay sincere about it even if the rest of the group are cracking up around her.

'You should really be in our group,' she said. 'You're so clever. Compared to most of the shitheads in this place, hey. I mean, you don't say much, but you get good marks and that, don't you?'

'I do okay.' I fell in with this idea of 'cleverness'-equals-good-marks.

'Yeah, and you could look really great with a bit of work. Don't you reckon she could, Donna?'

Donna looked round blankly at me from where she was staring at James's group. The stare stayed on her face.

'I reckon so, anyway,' said Lisa. 'And I'm going to be a beautician, so I know all about, you know, bringing out the best in people. Like, their looks. You need to cut your hair so the curls'd spring up, you know?' She started fiddling with my hair.

'Aargh, get off!' I pushed her hands away, laughing, feeling myself go red.

'I mean it. It wouldn't take much. You should come round to my place and I'd make you over. I've got a friend who can cut hair. She's excellent. You'd look *so* good.'

'It gets in my eyes.'

'So? Is that the end of the *world*? Scared you won't be able to see the *whiteboard*?'

'I guess not.'

'You should think about it.'

And she was looking at me, *assessing my potential*, and I was seeing her close up for the first time. It's true, she has got perfect skin (not even a freckle) and eyes like Michelle Pfeiffer's set wide apart, and hair so bright it makes marks on your retinas when you look away.

Lisa's very beautiful. That's why everyone does what she says, girl or boy. You can't believe this *vision*, this girl who should be a model, is actually focusing on you, is speaking to you. I remember my astonishment, even if I don't feel it now. Or I felt, *Gee*,

28

why's she bothering with all this? How can somebody who looks so good not just rise above us all? Why hasn't she been talent-scouted away from us? Why, oh why? The sound of her giggles up the back of the room makes me feel sick, and just the sight of her hair, clipped or tied or wound up differently every time you see her, turns me wooden and stupid even when she's on the other side of the playground, even if she's walking away from me.

You never see her on her own, always in a huddle with Donna and those other girls. They get a look on their faces, the whole group, and they swagger around spattering fear generally until Donna decides who to pick on next; then they come in for the kill. They're terrifying, and whoever hangs out with them becomes terrifying. *I* used to be terrifying! Little invisible Mel!

Being part of Lisa's group gives you power. You see it the way kids look at you, move out of your way, think about what they say to you. When you stop being in the group it's different: they all close in and push at you again, and their voices are contemptuous, glad you're on the outer, a victim, like them.

I smell Oriana before I see her—some strong, headachey, sweet perfume. It's like a wind rolling down Pug's stairs; it almost flattens my hair.

She's sitting on Pug's bed fiddling with her fingernails, claws applied at a salon. She's wearing a red suit, short and very tight, and she's got so much hair, like hundreds of black corkscrews bursting out of her head; she crowds the room with her hair and her perfume.

She looks up at me from under viciously plucked brows. 'Hi, I'm Dino's sister. Oriana. You've gotta be Mel.'

'Yes.'

'He's just takin' a leak. Won't be a minute. How ya doin'?' She shifts on the bed to indicate I should sit down.

'Oh, not bad.' The scent ripples as I push into it.

She looks me over again. 'You're doin' Year 12, Dino says.' I nod. 'What ya hangin' out with him for, then? Nah, just joking.

He's about the smartest one in our family.' She snorts. 'Not that *that's* saying much.' Pug comes in. 'Your girlfriend's here,' Oriana says flatly, watching his face light up as he sees me.

'Thought you weren't gunna get here 'til four o'clock!' He kisses my cheek like a husband.

'I took the last lesson off.'

'Good on you. I mean, it wasn't anything important, was it?'

'Sport.'

Oriana chuckles. 'He's like that with you too, huh? Used to always be on at me about jigging school. Does 'e check your homework, too?' She dodges his swinging foot. 'Hey, don't mess me up!'

'Mess you up? You do a good enough job of that yourself,' he says kindly. 'You don't need me.'

'Yes I do.' She picks up a tiny black patent handbag hardly big enough to hold a tampon, and stands up decisively, pulling her red skirt down all round. 'Don't forget to talk to Dad about what I told you, okay Dino?'

'Yeah, okay.'

She blows him a kiss and waves at me. '*Ciao.*'

'*Ciao,*' answers Pug.

'See you.' When she's gone I blink and flap a hand in front of my face. 'Boy, that is some pong!'

'Yeah,' Pug grins. 'She overdoes everything, my sister.'

'She's friendly enough.'

'Yeah. Careful what you say to her, but. She's a real motor-mouth. Like, she's probably ringing my mum up right now to say she's met you.'

'It's okay. I didn't let anything slip. So what do you have to talk to your dad about?'

'Oh, don't ask,' he groans. 'Whether she can stay out later, some shit. She wants me to work on the old man.'

'Must be handy, having siblings.'

'It's a bloody nuisance, if you ask me.'

'What does she do for *you*, in return?'

'For me? Nothing. Oh, she buys me awful stuff for Christmas. *Clothes*, you know, that cost a bloody arm and a leg and make me look like an idiot. I mean, you seen what she wears. Same stuff, only for guys. Stuff to go to *discos* in,' he finishes witheringly.

'Very you.' I'm enjoying seeing him uncomfortable, entangled in his family. Perhaps it wouldn't be so bad to meet the rest of them? No, no, no. Me in a houseful of Orianas? I'd fade away to nothing, turn into a piece of wood, a skirting board or a broom handle, something completely mundane and invisible. There's not enough of me to hold out against the personalities; I don't have a strong enough smell.

Scene: Lisa's bedroom. LISA and ME sit at opposite ends of her bed,
LISA painting fingernails.
ME: Lees, do you ever look at your hands and wonder if they belong to you?
LISA: Uh, no, Mel, I can't say I do. *(Shoots are-you-losing-it look at ME.)*
ME: Like, do you ever wonder how they got to be these hands, your hands, from just being little fat baby hands, same as everyone else's?
LISA *(shooting another look)*: Um, never had a problem with that, Mel. You feeling okay?
(They both laugh, releasing LISA's built-up puzzlement.)
ME: I mean it! Don't you see them doing things in front of you and just think, 'It's amazing! What's behind all this? Who *told* them to move like that? How did they know to grow into these skinny, bony . . .' *(Waves hands to show, lost for words.)*
LISA: You've got nice hands. *(Snort of laughter.)* Your head's a bit weird, but your hands are fine. *(Looks proprietorially over at them.)* You keep your nails too short, and you could moisturise more often, but basically, good hands.

31

ME: You're hopeless. You've missed the point completely.
(Falls back across pillows, giving up.)
LISA: Well, when you go and get all religious on me . . . *(looks up, spreads hands, polish brush held delicately)* . . . well, who wants to know, babe?

A condom spilling honey, a streak down the door where it was pushed through the ventilation slots, drizzling down a pile of new textbooks. I feel eyes through the after-school scramble, a silence at the far end of the locker aisle. *There is no honey*, I tell myself. *There is no condom.* I pack my bag, maintain the rhythm of packing as I grab up the sticky condom in some tissues and stuff it into the bag as well. I close the locker door and leave, past bent backs shaking with giggles.

I always get Pug to tell me how he's spent his week—he used not to be able to remember, but now he tries really hard—he thinks it's really funny that I'm interested. He'll be up to *Tuesday* and he'll say 'You don't wanna hear about this boring shit!' He can't believe me when I say I do, and force him to go on about the latest feud in the Magnini family, or the fight he saw Thursday night.

Always after spending time with Pug I feel like coming home and writing everything down, to hang on to the feeling. Our house is so boring, so not-happy, so flat, and when I'm over at Pug's I seem to be all-over alive, awake as I never am at home—brain and body both. He looks in my eyes as if he wants to suck my brain out through them.

I just enjoy touching him, walking down grotty old Erskineville Road or somewhere, his hand in my back jeans pocket, his voice in my ear. Living in a family is so *un-sexy*—how does it get to be like this? It had to start off better, didn't it? Mum's told me about it. She sounded as if she was in love with Dad, back then. Why does that seem so ridiculous now? Definitely those two are *not* in love. I wouldn't even say they love each other. I wouldn't say either of them are crazy about *me*, even. We remind me of three trains running side by side along parallel tracks. We never look at each other, we hardly touch, we never do anything together, unless you count the supermarket shopping—whoopee. We never talk more than we have to: 'Can I go on the excursion, Mum?' 'Sure. Here's $10'. It's weird, when you think about it. Are all families like this?

Lisa's isn't. Her dad's a really hearty type, always making rude jokes that crack her mum up and make Lisa and Troy *groan*. They're always hugging each other and pushing each other and tickling and carrying on. At least, when I knew them they were; it's a while since I checked. Loudmouth Lisa, ex-best friend.

The Lewises are okay, too. They don't make as much noise as the Wilkinsons, but you can tell they're *joined*. They all run together on the same track instead of four different ones, all going along when Josh's playing hockey or Ambra's in the swimming sports. I'd be lucky to get Mum to the school once a year on Prize Night, and Dad—well, you don't want to know, do you, Dad? I only mention kids at school every now and again, but when I do you switch on the lectures about being an individual (a good little train running alone down the line) and not being led by the crowd. God, if only there *was* a crowd to be led by! There is *no-one*, honestly. I can say without anyone contradicting me, *I have no friends at school* any more. I used to have friends. I used to have a boyfriend there, even. I used to love getting up and going to school. Every evening I'd be on the phone with someone, organising for the weekend. I went out every Friday and Saturday night for nearly a whole year.

And the years before that, school was different. There were gang-like groups, but they didn't have much power, and they didn't have decisive leaders like Donna-and-Lisa or James Li. New people came and changed the whole mood of the school, and other people left, like (most importantly) Natalie Begley, who was my friend and went to London with her dad. And there were also a few sensible people like Russell Daice—small, clever and very good at dissolving disagreements, so sure of himself, but so nice about it, that no-one could put him down. People like him were an antidote to all the jocks, but now there's no resistance, and the jocks and the victimisers charge around doing what they please. Everything is likely to slip out of control there at any moment—last year some classes came so close to rioting it wasn't funny, though I pretended it was at the time.

I was pretty sure I was happy, last year—I'd never hung around with such a lot of people, felt so popular. It was hard keeping up the pace, but it was exciting being there when rules (spoken and unspoken), sometimes real *laws*, were being breached. I didn't actually lead any break-ins, but I went for joy-rides in a few stolen cars, and picked up a few 'bargains' from the shops around King Street with Lisa. It was terrifying, but at least I felt awake; I wasn't waiting for something to happen, as it'd felt like for all my life up until then.

Well, now it's all shot to pieces, isn't it? I'd rather be in a coma than in this state of fearful *super*-awareness all the time, watching the shreds of everything I had last year fall through my fingers. Sometimes, when things are really black, Pug seems like a kind of consolation prize for having lost everything else in the bomb blast. *Here, have this unemployed bruiser*, someone said, and tossed him to me.

But I dropped the bomb myself, didn't I? Can't blame anyone else. I opened the bomb-bay doors (my mouth) and pressed the release button and, plop!, the bomb (the words) landed right in Lisa's lap. Then she took it to school and laid it in the middle of the playground and detonated it. Blammo! Everything I'd had at that place was gone.

I *hate* that girl. She's *evil* for doing that. (I'm crying; I can't believe I'd let them make me cry. It must be PMS. It's about that time, I think. It must be.) But I should've known I'd get it wrong. After four years sitting quietly with Natalie in a corner of the yard, of course everyone knew I was pretending when I started

34

cutting loose with Donna and Lisa. Now I figure they all saw through me. They just sat around waiting for me to blow it, and it was only a matter of time before I did. Nobody told me that if something stupid happens to you, like getting pregnant, you *don't* tell your best friend, if she's a 'best friend' like Lisa. I should've been able to see that—if I hadn't been pretending, if I hadn't wanted friends so badly that she wheedled the story out of me, if I hadn't been trying to impress her with how experienced I was, if I'd bloody well *thought about it*! I mean, I knew that Lisa, underneath the dizzy surface she uses, is a really hard person, really judgemental. Sometimes she turns on the charm and sometimes she turns on the freezer. I remember (it hurts) how she tried to keep the charm going when I started telling her. Suddenly we were both acting. We weren't best friends any more—some security wall, like they have in banks, had shot up between us. On one side she was staring, her eyes hard with dislike, her brain whirring; on the other side I was spitting it out, gobbet after gobbet, the stuff of juicy gossip.

I managed to stop myself before I named Brenner. I managed to not say a few things when she turned on me and asked. I stopped and sat perfectly still, biting my lips closed.

Then suddenly she remembered she had to go home 'to help her mum'. And as she was going I said 'This is just between us, right, Lisa?' as fiercely as I could, but it was too late. 'Sure,' she said, and looked away. She was already freezing over. 'See you later.'

Yeah well, *see* you later, but we haven't *spoken* to each other since. I thought it'd die down over Christmas, but this year is worse than ever. The looks I get! That awful feeling when anyone who finds themselves near you immediately starts inching away. It's foul! I keep my head down and work, trying to focus my panicking brain, come home, collapse on the bed, and when I wake up do homework, watch TV, try not to think about the next day unless the next day's Saturday or Sunday. Weekend memories keep me strong for the first couple of days before desperation for the *next* weekend takes over. Sometimes on a Friday I think I'm really going to crack up. There's a really wild feeling at our school on Friday—everybody's stirred up and practically partying already. Fridays I can't tell whether people are going to leave me alone or come on extra strong to counteract their boredom. I mean, Mondays I *know* Brenner'll be in a foul mood and Lisa'll be hung over and Donna freezer-faced and powermongery, but Fridays I just *can't tell*. All day I have to watch my back, and when I get home . . . the relief, the freedom—it's dizzying.

We went to the clinic, Mum and I. Outside, after the counselling, a clutch of people flaunted aborted-foetus placards. One caught my eye and mourned, '*Don't* kill your baby!'

'Take no notice,' Mum said when we got out of earshot. 'A person's entitled to a choice.'

I thought about the person inside me, who next week wouldn't even exist. *No, not person. Not baby*. Growth, to be excised, like a fibroid. Humungous anxiety, to be removed. Or so I thought, before I'd opened the bomb bay.

I jig school at lunchtime to go to Pug's. It's too easy; I just wait until the teacher on yard duty's up the other end and walk out. I'm trembling with my own daring, ducking home to change. I'm just so *sure* someone will see me and ask where I'm going, and dob me in to Mum and Dad. But I make it over there okay. Pug is out, but one of the other guys, Joe, lets me in. I go upstairs, lie on Pug's bed and wait.

When he gets back he looks at me all cold and alien from training. 'What's happened?'

I don't mean to whisper, but that's how it comes out. 'Nothing.' Then I try again and say in a proper voice, 'Nothing's happened.'

He sits down next to me. 'You don't look too good.'

'It's the light through the leaves. All green.'

'No, *sad*, not sick. What's eatin' ya?' He takes my hands.

And I just go to pieces. Him saying 'sad' is what does it. Yes, I *am* sad; yes, something *is* eating me. God knows what—everything! I cry and lie and say it's all the sneaking around.

'But do you really have to be sneaky?' says Pug, lying down next to me. 'I mean, we're goin' together, aren't we? Are we?'

'I guess . . . I guess we are.' It's the first time I've actually said it.

'I'm not seeing any other girl. Haven't since a while before I met you; you know all about that. And you're not sneakin' round behind some other bloke's back, or anything. It's just your parents.'

'Yeah.'

'Well, you could tell your parents.'

Sure I could. You'd be delighted, wouldn't you, parents dear? *What an oaf*, you'd say to each other in your room that night. Where'd she get *him*?

'What, they'd reckon I wasn't good enough for you?' His face is right up close to mine, our noses touching. His eyes are just a blurry sparkle.

Aagh. Yeah, they would reckon that, but that's not the problem. It's something about *me*, and what *I'd* reckon. Eventually I just say, 'Yes, something like that.'

After sparkling for a long time, he says, 'They'd be right, you know.' His voice is really hushed, as if he's telling me some terrible secret.

He's dead serious. He's so serious and so close that my throat shuts off and I don't breathe for a few seconds. I nearly say *I love you*—which I vowed I'd never say to anyone again! Instead I nod and stick out my tongue like a snake's to touch his nose. 'Wrong side of the tracks, boy,' I laugh. A leftover tear sneaks across into my other eye.

'I am. I am,' he insists. 'Is that okay with you?'

'What d'you mean? I was just joking, you idiot.'

He shakes his head. 'Yeah, well, I reckon one day you're not gunna joke about it.'

I move my head back to see him better. 'What are you on about?' I say uncomfortably.

He watches my mouth, speaks carefully. 'I just reckon, you know, someone like you . . . you'll, you know, move on and that.'

'"Like me"? What's that?'

'Well . . . smart enough to stay in school. There's that. And, well, your mum and dad, both working. With office jobs and that, I mean.'

'My dad's a salesman. An insurance salesman. That's not exactly high class, is it?'

'Higher than a car mechanic, like my dad. Higher than unemployed, like me. He'd wear a suit to work, wouldn't he?'

'I don't understand,' I say. 'You're judging *me* by who my *parents* are. When it's about you and me, here in this room.'

'No.' He lies on his back. 'This is nice, but it's not everything.'

'It's everything we need to think about now.'

He stares at the festoons of dust on the ceiling rose. 'I'm not talkin' about now. I'm talkin' about later on.'

'Why? What's wrong with now, that you have to go glooming on about the future?' Says I, the one who was just crying my eyes out about *everything*.

'Nothing,' he says quickly, and faces me again. 'Nothing, except . . . I don't want it to finish.'

'It's *not* finishing!'

'But it will.' Finally his eyes meet mine and stay.

I can't bluster any more. 'Maybe,' I say in a low voice.

He looks sad, and satisfied in a way. I feel as if he's tortured a confession out of me, but I'm not sure how much I've given away.

'But *now*,' I insist, my hands pressing his back.

'Yeah? Now?'

'Now I love you,' I say to his chest.

'Okay.' He begins to smile, to pull me closer. 'Let's forget about later on, then.'

'Let's.' I laugh with relief.

At three weeks the embryonic cells are beginning to differentiate themselves. The first stages of a rudimentary brain are a swelling at one end; the embryo's outermost cells are early nerves. Inside, bones, muscles, blood vessels, organs and a simple intestinal tube are beginning to form.

'Coming to the shops with us tomorrow night?' says Mum over Wednesday dinner. 'I thought we could go on to Pasha's afterwards.'

'Working late tomorrow. Sorry.'

Mum puts on a groan. 'We hardly ever see you.'

Dad: 'Gotta be done.'

'I didn't drag you up by your bootstraps just so you'd disappear from our lives.' She's looking at me, winking, when Dad's knife crashes onto his plate.

'Bloody hell!' he roars. 'What a thing to say! And in front of Mel, too. Whatever I've done—'

'It was just a joke, Dave—' she mutters, startled.

'Whatever I've achieved I've achieved by the sweat of my own bloody brow, not because *you*—'

'It was a *joke*, for crying out loud! *Mel* knows it's not true, *I* know it's not true, *you* know—'

'—not because of *anything* you did!' He finishes and they stare at each other.

'Hey, calm down, you guys.' My voice sounds insultingly mild and weak.

But Mum's picked up on something. 'Well, *moral* support doesn't count for anything, I guess?' she says rather coldly.

Dad goes back to his dinner.

'Or *practical* support, I suppose? Like, four years of being on the night shift with Mel? That wasn't of any assistance to you?'

After a nasty pause, Dad rolls his eyes. 'Yeah, right, Jan, you've been a saint. Now drop it.' I've never heard him be rude to Mum like this.

'*You* brought it up, remember.' She stands up. Her eyes are filling with tears. She stacks my empty plate on hers, then snatches Dad's from under his nose.

'Hey, I'm not finished!'

'If you want to eat, you can make your own bloody tea!' She takes the plates out, leaving Dad looking stupid with his knife and fork in his hands. He glances at me, as if to check whether I noticed.

'You've really hurt her.' There's surprise in my voice, as if I hadn't thought it was possible.

'Huh! She put the boot in first!'

'She asked you out. That's what happened *first*.'

He stares at me as if I were a piece of furniture that decided to sit up and talk. 'Bloody women!' he mutters, putting down his cutlery. He gets up and goes over to the television.

'Bloody men!' I retort in a boofhead voice just before he switches on.

Scene: Franklins. MUM and ME are cruising through the meat section.

ME: So *did* you drag Dad up by his bootstraps?

MUM: I cut the ad out of the paper, that's all. I helped him buy the suit for the interview, made him get his hair cut. It was a joke we had, that I made him do it. Until the other night, that is.

ME: What's up with him?

MUM: I don't know. Midlife crisis. *(Look at each other, ME questioning, MUM not having any answers. MUM draws a breath, looks bright.)* How about Chinese, after?

ME *(not hungry at all)*: Yeah, good idea.

Lunch at Pug's parents' place. Two short bundles, one of loud anger, one of smiling serenity, plus three tall children—snappy Lu, understated Dino and exotic Oriana, a big exclamation mark pining for an exciting sentence to justify its existence. That's the Magninis, and as a combo they're pretty hair-raising for someone from a single-child Anglo family. Where's the volume control? Where's the OFF switch? Even when they're just having normal conversations they sound as if they're fighting; when they're fighting, they make enough noise for ten people. All of a sudden I get an inkling of why Pug took up boxing—the blissful quiet of fighting without words.

It's a three-way conflict between Oriana, Mr Magnini and Pug's older brother Luciano. Mrs Magnini throws in the odd placating remark, trying to draw attention back to the enormous, rich lunch she's cooked, and Pug rolls his eyes at all the noise and provides brief translations for me. Towards dessert he starts getting fed up with them.

'*Basta, basta!*' he yells over the three of them, so suddenly I jump. The noise stops, the room rings. He scowls from father to brother to sister, then goes on to say something very emphatic, with a lot of arm-waving, indicating me with his hands, indicating them, himself. When he stops, his father looks at me, waves his fork at Luciano. 'Sorry. My son can't help, he is an idiot.' Oriana hoots and Luciano laughs and retorts something.

'Shut up, Lu,' says Pug.

'Sorry.' Luciano pretends to be ashamed of himself, then winks across at me.

We get through to coffee before the next eruption. For a while Mr Magnini puts up with Luciano's goading, greeting it with a haughty look, a puff of air, a wave of a large hand. Then Luciano hits some sore spot and he can't stay silent any more. Back and forth they go; it's like watching a tennis match.

Pug reaches across and picks up my coffee in its little gilt cup and saucer. 'Come on, Mel, let's leave 'em to it.'

I follow him onto the patio, which is pebblecreted with a white balustrade and two ornate concrete pots spilling red geraniums. A vegetable garden marches away down the yard, and a tiny white concrete fountain in the shape of a semi-nude goddess spills into its bowl on the strip of left-over lawn.

It's a relief to see sky instead of black flock curlicues on a gold paper background, instead of fancy-cut crystal glass and gold cutlery and lace tablecloth. It's great to breathe air instead of pasta-steam and chicken-steam and garlic-onion-and-rosemary steam, to feel the nausea-block in my throat easing back in the eerie quietness.

I steady my saucer on the iron-lace table. 'Is it always this bad?'

'Oh, yeah, about. Usually I haven't got any excuse to dip out, but.' Pug smiles at me, shamefaced. 'Yeah. Sometimes it can get heavy, you know, Dad laying down the law and Lu and Oriana just blowing up. Once he decides on something, he won't bloody shift.'

'And what about you? Don't you ever blow up at him?'

'Well, just then was about . . . yeah, that'd be about the most noise I ever make.'

'What were you saying to them? I was impressed.'

Pug looks at his runners tapping on the terracotta tiles. 'I told them they should be ashamed of 'mselves. I said, "I've brung this girl along specially to meet you. What's she going to think? What's she going to tell her parents? That we're a bunch of crazy wogs who can't control their tempers? She'll leave me, listening to you lot. She won't want to have anything to do with me."'

'You idiot.'

'Well, at least they'll get off my back now, about meeting you. Aah, they're all right. Take 'em one by one and they're fine. It's just in a group they start actin' like animals.'

Among the photos on top of the television, an old one of Luciano, Dino and Oriana in a row. 'Oh, this's *you*!' I say, grabbing it up.

'Yeah, in the middle.' Pug's arms go around my waist, his chin onto my shoulder.

'Oh well, I knew *that*!' Putting him down is a way to cover up the sudden—oof! What is it? A throb of anguish, a knot tightening, a terrible *reaction*. His younger sister is just plain innocent, a happy little kid, nothing to worry about; Luciano is cocky and self-important in his little brown suit. Between them my crew-cut, big-eared Pug seems to beam out sweetness; it's his wide eyes, and his being just a *tiny* bit self-conscious, not hugely, like his brother, or completely unaware like Oriana. That smile: sort of I-know-I-ought-to-smile, sort of I'm-just-enjoying-myself-anyway. Part of me wants to kidnap this photo, take it off public view, keep it all to myself; part of me wants never to have seen it. Because I can see how Pug was wide open for the world to blunder into, and it did, and I'm going to get flashes of this face (I've already had them!) as long as ever I know him, and with every flash this twist inside.

Dad said, 'God, remember how nice this street used to be?' We were driving to Grandma's, I remember. I looked out the window. It looked okay to me. Just houses, quite neat. Someone had a pair of small concrete lions either side of their gate, which I thought was a cool idea.

'All the big trees are gone,' said Mum.

'Well, you wouldn't want roots buggering up your pebblecrete, would you? Look at it, it's been woggified to death.'

'Da-ave!'

'Well, it has—look, colonnades everywhere! Statues, aluminium windows.' He shuddered. 'Used to be nice old cottages all along here.'

'People have different tastes, that's all. Give 'em a break.'

At four and a half weeks the embryo looks like a prehistoric animal. Rudimentary heart and eyes have formed, as has a tail, which will disappear within weeks, leaving shrunken tail-bones as a permanent reminder of humankind's animal past.

Nobody brought Pug and me together, like Lisa engineering a whole bunch of matches at that party (me and Brenner, Kerry and Cory Worth, Anna and Toby) just to see if she could do it. It just happened. When I think how easily Pug could've just walked on past it's really a bit scary.

It was a week or so after the miscarriage. I went up to Newtown to look for Christmas presents because I wanted to enjoy myself, but I couldn't find anything, and halfway through looking I had a weird attack of . . . I don't know. The bottom dropped out of my emotions and I fell through. Everything looked *bad*— Newtown grungy and full of nightmare people, all *weird* one way or another, no-one smiling, the shops pathetic little temples of greed, the humidity pressing in, the traffic a herd of mad animals funnelling between the buildings. Worst of all was my life. I hadn't heard from Brenner all week. It was the day after I'd told Lisa, and I *knew* that was a *bad* stuff-up. I was floundering, horrified at her having wormed most of my story out of me—I could hear her sweet, calculating voice in my head and my own confiding one, see her eyes swivelling away from me. I'd gone too far and I was petrified of what she was going to do. I stood outside Coles Fosseys looking in at the bundles of tinsel, sweating embarrassment and fear.

I struggled on for a bit, but then I thought, *Stuff it, I'll go home, go to bed and sleep this off.* So I turned down Mary Street.

And almost straight away I regretted it, but not quite soon enough to retreat. Four guys straggled across the path and the road, all in top spirits, yelling and pushing at each other. I tried to look invisible and not-caring at the same time.

But—clunk!—they saw me.

One whistled and shouted 'G'day, gorgeous!' at me. I crossed to the other footpath and he crossed too. He was grinning and glancing at his mates.

'Keep out of my way,' I said, really *severe*.

He dodged about in front of me, wouldn't let me pass. 'Can't take a compliment, this one. Come on, gorgeous, loosen up. What's your name, love?'

'Get away!' I sort of choked. I saw his hand come out. *'Don't you touch me!'*

He patted me on the shoulder and let his hand drop. 'Look me in the face, love. Ask me nicely.' A real soft, nasty voice.

'Lay off, Ed,' one of the mates said warningly—that was Pug.

'Just want her to be polite to a guy, mate.'

I hissed through my teeth at him. 'Get out of my way, *shithead*.' Any second I was going to attack him!

He dropped his jaw. 'Now, that's not very nice, is it?'

'E-ed.' His mate was a step closer, the other two hanging back and watching.

I felt myself going off my brain. 'Did I ask for your stupid whistling, your *"compliments"*? I was just walking down the *street*, for God's sake. You guys all think you're God's bloody gift, don't you? Think every girl's just *hanging out* for compliments! Well, we're not! We couldn't give a *stuff* what jerks like you think!'

'It's okay,' said the other guy at my shoulder. 'Ed, fuck off now, hey?' But I was just as angry at him! I didn't want his stupid *protection*!

'What's *she* getting so upset about? She's not so great-looking anyway. No tits, no nothing.' Ed started sidling off.

I yelled at him, 'Who *cares*, you moron? Better than having no *brain*!' My knees were shaking with rage, and I had to *charge* past him up the street so he wouldn't see.

'Geez, you're a dickhead, Ed!' I heard the mate say.

After a pause to think, Ed yelled back, 'Geez, you're a wimp, Dino!'

'Hey—' Pug was catching me up.

'And you can bugger off, too!' I said to him. I just wanted to get away before the tears started, didn't want *any* of them to see me crying.

'It's okay. I don't want to hassle you. I just don't want you to let that fuckwit get to you.'

I couldn't see him through tears *vrooming* up to my eyes. '*You're* the fuckwit, hanging out with such a jerk . . .' My voice gave out and I had to face the fact that I was crying.

'Really he's okay. He just goes stupid when there's girls around.'

When there are *girls around, idiot.*

I had to wait at the corner of Lennox Street for cars to pass, and the shaking came up from my knees and took over; I gasped and sniffed and wanted to be somewhere all on my own where I could howl as loudly as I wanted. Instead I licked up the tears and slimed the back of my wrist with my nose. 'Oh, go *away*,' I told him as he started crossing the road with me. 'For God's *sake*!'

'Hey, sit down for a minute, eh.' He pointed to a park bench. I nearly tripped over the edge of the path, and he touched my elbow to steady me. 'Come on, you can't hardly see where you're goin'.'

He sat down at the other end of the bench, which I guess was better than standing over me, but I still wished he wasn't there. I was ashamed of cracking up—I just wanted to get *away*.

I was mopping at my face with a been-through-the-wash tissue I'd found in my pocket when he spoke again.

'You don't want to take any notice of Ed. He's a *immature* bastard. Doesn't know when to stop.'

'Pretty hard *not* to take notice, when he's parked right there in your *way*,' I pointed out.

'Yeah. Sorry. He just goes stupid, like I said.'

He was trying really hard to make things better. I remember thinking what a *serious* person he seemed, in spite of the fact that he could hardly string a sentence together.

I can still call him up from then. He had a neat haircut—neat as in short and neat as in cool, and he *wasn't* wearing a back-to-front baseball cap like the other three *dudes*. His black hair gleamed in the sunshine. His face—well, the memory of his face is all mixed up now with seeing his face in other sorts of places and lights and ways, but the eyes stuck with me, so pale, and the lashes and eyebrows so dark. He looked so clean, somehow, and cool, in spite of the steamy weather—I was damp all over, not just around the eyes. I noticed how fit he was, too, not puffed-up muscle like a gym junkie or anything, but I remember staring at his shoulders and arms, following the curves of them.

'It's just that I wasn't expecting it, that's all,' I said. 'And, you know, some days you wake up feeling strong, and some days you just can't cope with things like that.'

He nodded without looking at me. I saw a little smile on the side of his face. 'I dunno. You coped okay, I reckon.'

'Huh. He still didn't move out of my way, did he?'

'I thought you were gunna take a swipe at 'im!' he laughed.

'I was! I should've! Mind you, he could've hit me back harder.'

'Nah, he'd've been too shocked. Anyway, he wouldn't hit a girl. Even Ed's not that much of an arsehole.'

I didn't know what to think of that. It was sexist, but a different kind of sexism from the kind I was used to at school. It was kind of old-fashioned, gentlemanly, kind of a *bearable* sexism. Again, he was perfectly serious about it.

Then he looked at me and we both smiled, and there was a connection there, and as the smiles tailed off I thought, *That's not all. Something else has to happen yet.*

There was a pause. 'I'd better get on home,' I said unwillingly, testing the feeling I'd just had.

'I was hoping you'd let me buy you a coffee, or a cold drink or sumpthink.'

'What, to help me get over the shock?' I joked.

'Nah.' He looked at me over his shoulder. 'We could talk some more.'

Suddenly the episode with Ed didn't matter any more, except that it had led us up to this point, this meeting-point.

'Okay.' I kept my voice light, just in case nothing should come of it. But of course, something did. A whole *lot* did.

That meeting-day we were just friendly. He was so *polite*, that was what felt so good. And careful and kind. I wasn't used to it. I was used to keeping up with Brenner, who sometimes paid compliments just to watch my face go all soft with gratitude, then snatched the compliment back and laughed at me. 'Just joking! Geez, you're so *sen*-sitive!', like it was a major fault in me.

Another thing, Pug didn't seem to be busting to get back to his mates. I kept waiting for him to make some excuse to get up and go, and he kept *staying*, and asking more questions. He hardly said anything about himself. He told me later he was embarrassed about having no job, and thought I'd disapprove about the boxing. He made me talk, though. He sat still and took me seriously. He listened and asked questions and didn't make a single judgemental comment. I found myself saying things I hadn't known I thought, drawn out by his interest. I found myself not having to bother about seeming cool or sophisticated, not having to worry about getting my tone right. I could just mag on, yarn on, take things back and restate them, disagree with myself. It was great.

For a while we had a casual kind of relationship. We only saw each other every week or so, and hardly ever left his room when we did. School got worse, and our meetings started to be the only nice times I had, and then the Christmas holidays started. God, was that an orgy of lies and sex! My 'best friend' Lisa was very handy during that time—even when she was away I could go for 'long walks' to 'mope' and 'miss her'. That was when I really got to know Pug, seeing him almost every day. Pavement-sizzling afternoons, jacaranda-blue skies, pollution and bushfire smoke souring the streets, sunshine stinging: we sheltered in the shadowy must of that room in the share house, talking, sleeping, *being* together for hours. He turned out to be not quite so serious *all* the time as I first thought, but he is basically a serious and careful person, wrongly packaged in a boxer's body. That's when I got addicted to him, started seeing the point of sex, started realising what a dud Brenner had been.

Going back to school meant major deprivation after that. But if I didn't have Pug I don't know how I'd cope with all the school stuff—he gives me enough of a boost to keep me grinding on, day after day, walking there, weathering whatever, walking back, sitting at my desk working. He thinks it's very important, me doing the HSC, more important than *I* think it is, because I can't see what it's going to lead to. Haven't a clue; don't much care. It's just . . . it's there, and it seems slightly more pointless to stop than it does to go on. So I do.

I walk past Lisa and Kerry and Jasper Sceates at the bus stop. I'm halfway past and there's deadly silence when Lisa sings out, 'Well, hullo Melanie!'

There's that teasing look in her eye. I just want to be far, far away, but I don't speed up or anything. I give her a blank look, a Donna look, and go on past. I don't say *anything*—I can just hear how she'd parrot it back at me.

They fall about laughing behind me. Jasper calls out, 'Stackin' on the weight a bit, aren't ya?' and the two girls shush him and Lisa says in a false voice, 'Jasper! Don't be so *cruel*!'

Stacking on the weight—I've never been bonier! Maybe that's all he means, the opposite of what he said. But the way Lisa and Kerry reacted . . .

Well, stuff Jasper Sceates as well. Stuff all of them. Forget about them. Think about Pug, how he looks at you, how much you matter.

Because there was only me, and I was quiet and good, Dad took me places. I perched in the cabs of bulldozers, doodled on memo pads in factory offices, played with kittens in other people's houses while above me Dad knitted deals with his talk of premiums and no-claim bonuses, fire, injury and acts of God. I was patient, too;

I learned patience going out with Dad, being in a new place, exploring it to death, then putting in another hour until he was ready to go.

In some people's faces you can see what they looked like as children, or the old people they'll be, when the flesh padding has sagged and shrunk and the bones show through. With some people you can't see far. I could imagine Lisa, for example, as a pretty child (she did show me photos, too), but I couldn't imagine her any older. Mind you, she never stopped moving and talking—her face was hard to concentrate on because I cared so much what it was doing; I had to think about my own reactions all the time and get them right. I remember I had a hard time seeing Brenner sometimes, squinting through my image of him as a leathery old lifesaver striding *manfully* about on the beach, silly red-and-yellow cap tied under his chin. With Pug I can't tell. He is just Pug *now*, that is, *as* I see him, *inside the moment* I'm seeing him in. I get so fixated on the details of him sometimes it's hard to step back far enough to *see* his complete face, let alone reshape it in my imagination as a baby's, as a man Dad's age.

With my own face, it's hopeless, too: a small face with too many odd, over-sized features crammed into it. When I see my face after looking at others it seems too convex, everything too curly: a mouth quirked into a kind of weird permanent smile, black eyebrows making flourishes over my eyes, a great tassel of wavy black hair, thick enough to swing me from. Everything off-balance, out of proportion.

And this *bosom* that's growing on me's the same; the rest of my body seems to be stretching out and getting thinner like a piece of chewing gum, while it swells and hurts and tingles and gets bumped and elbowed, because I'm not used to it yet; I forget where it ends.

I can't tell where I'll go, how I'll change, what I'm going to look like next month, next year. I look and wonder, waiting for something to finish developing and start deteriorating so I can know, so I can relax.

Speaking of tension, I'm wound up with waiting for something else. I always feel as if I'm right on the verge of getting a period, but it's been weeks, and one hasn't come. I've had so many scares before, though, and they didn't amount to anything. And the one time I *should've* been scared I didn't feel a thing, didn't even think until I was two months overdue, so . . .

Scene. LISA and ME at school, at edge of group.

LISA: You're one of those pale people.

ME: Sure. Sickly pale.

LISA: Pale and *mysterious*. Like, you look kind of foreign, you know?

ME: Chinese? Tongan? Eskimo?

LISA *(punching MY arm)*: Don't be *dumb*. Like *French* or something! Like you ought to be wrapped up in furs in a carriage.

ME: Instead of slobbing round in jeans and a T-shirt in Newtown? Sounds good to me. Show me a fur and I'll throw it on.

LISA *(looking thoughtful)*: No, I'm just trying to home in, you know?, to your colours.

ME *(looking down at clothes and pretending to be shocked)*: What, blue denim and frayed grey cotton *aren't* my colours?

LISA: They're everyone's colours, so everyone looks like a nobody in them. You want something that's going to make you stand out.

ME *(doubtfully)*: I do?

Six weeks after fertilisation, extremely short arms and legs are visible. The red blob in the chest, a tiny heart, now beats about 150 times a minute, twice as fast as the mother's. The eyes and brain can be seen easily. The embryo's own blood supply, separate from its mother's, is piggybacked onto it by the placenta,

allowing the input of nutrients and the disposal of the embryo's
waste products. This second month of gestation is a sensitive time:
even slight defects in the embryo can bring on miscarriage.

Sometimes my eyes get stuck out of focus on a particular spot
and I really have to *wrench* them back, *make* myself move them
around. This happens a lot when I'm trying to study. Study's the
worst thing. I write and write and write and read and read and
read and *nothing* stays in my head. I got that History essay done,
but it took the *longest time*. It was like trying to get a really dense,
jumpy sheep through a really small gate. My thoughts just kept
slithering and racing away. Hopeless. But one thing I have, without all these friends *bothering* me, is time; time to herd that bloody
boring sheep through that and the dozen other bloody stupid
gates you have to get it through to be 'educated'.

Mum reckons while it's like this (not so stinking hot now, officially autumn, but still sunny) we should go down to the beach
house for a weekend. I don't know. It'd be nice, I guess; I mean,
it always is, but I don't want to leave town. I don't want to leave
Pug. We always manage to get together sometime every weekend,
and where would I be without my weekly ⊕⊖? In all other ways
I'd love to go. Christ, there's so *much* I'd like to get away from.
I'd *love* to have a Friday and a Monday off school, a *legitimate*
Friday or Monday, not a stolen one. But I think about a weekend
with my family, and about not seeing, not touching Pug at all for
two weeks straight (although I'd make it up somewhere, I'd lie,
I'd say I had to go out with Lisa) . . . I can't do it. *I don't want to.*

Dad doesn't seem all that keen either, which is a bit of a surprise. Usually he's busting to get down there and fiddle around
with fishing tackle or a boogie board. But he shrugs and says
'Maybe' in a dismissive, forget-it tone of voice, and Mum sighs
impatiently. 'What's *wrong* with you two? Mel, go and take an
iron tablet. You look as pale and peaky as a TB victim! You can't
tell me *you* don't need a break—up all night with your head in a

52

textbook!' I just went and took the tablet, and didn't go back. And nothing more's been said about going away since then, thank God. Don't make me do it, Mum, please, please, *please*.

'You look fabulous,' says Pug. He's taking my clothes off.

'It's as if you're opening a big present,' I laugh.

'Yeah, it's like that.'

A minute later, 'Never had a present that was wrapped up so complicated, but.'

I help him with the bra catch; the elastic's stretched as far as it'll go. I spill out—out, not down. I kind of sproing out, and suddenly I'm three centimetres closer to him. He puts both hands on me, and I feel as if I'll go bananas, those poor old squished nipples uncrinkling into his hands. I close my eyes and bite my lip and he sort of *groans* into my neck. We fall onto the bed and ⊕⊖ without even getting the bra right off; my underpants are around my knees and I don't know how he got in, but he did. *Easy.* Lovely boy. Lovely *man*, lovely man.

At seven weeks, brain cells begin to reach out and make contact with each other. Every minute, more than 100,000 new nerve cells are being created. The lobes of the cerebrum, where mental processes will take place and conscious activity will be decided, shine through the forehead skin, as yet unprotected by the cranium.

Less than 4 cm long and less than 15 grams in weight, at eight weeks the embryo possesses all its organs, all nearly fully formed. From now on they will become progressively more refined.

I meet Josh Lewis coming fast down our street.

'Hi, Josh.' I'm uncertain, thinking about Ambra.

He doesn't say anything. A thin arc of his white spit crosses my path.

A noise like 'pop!' comes from my mouth and I stagger. I call out after him, 'What was that for?'

He's walking away as if nothing's happened. What *has* happened? What does he know, or think he knows, to make him hate me? And who the hell else knows? I can hardly believe it, except for that splat on the path. It moves as the bubbles burst, like something alive.

> . . . as a means of self-defence it is wholly absurd . . . a light blow delivered to the testes can render a man as quickly *hors de combat*, flooring him and causing him to lose all further interest in fighting, but without doing him any permanent injury leading to darkness, imbecility or the grave.
>
> Yet the punch to the testes is barred and called a foul . . . while every wallop to the head and jaws, eyes, nose and ears, all of the delicate sensory organs, is hailed with delight and cheered, particularly when these blows bruise, maim, cut and tear.

Pug's first pro match is in two weeks up at the Youth Club. 'You gotta come,' he says. 'I want you to be there. You gotta see what it's all about.'

'You do? I do?' I suppose I do. See what all this training is for. I couldn't expect to watch rehearsals for ever, could I? I *did* expect it, though, when I consider.

Pug watches me hesitate. 'Come on, mate. It'd really make a difference if you came.'

So I say I will. Christ, I don't know how I'll get out on a week-night. Or whether I want to. I don't want to see Pug getting smacked in the head. If he could *guarantee* me a win, I'd go, no worries, but he won't say, won't talk about his chances. What if he's *creamed* in the first round, knocked flat? I can *see* it so easily! I can see him flat out on the canvas like a starfish. He'd look just like he does when he's asleep, only bloodier, only not private, not in the half-darkness under the frangipani, but out there under lights with the crowd howling and some bloody great *gorilla* standing over him. Everything in me says *Don't do it*, but Pug's committed now. In this part of his life I don't have a say. To accept, to watch, to support him whatever happens; my role's astonishingly clear. To keep my mouth shut on my own fears and tremblings, my own hysteria, to tell him he's the best, with conviction, even when we both know I'm lying.

God, how am I going to get away on that Thursday night? Like he says, I gotta. Whatever happens, I've got to be there to see.

Yes, there is a God. Dad's birthday, of course, the Sunday after the fight. Let's take dear Father down the coast for the weekend, Mum! *Brilliant* idea! We can muck around on the beach all weekend, and have a nice little family *party* on Sunday night. *Also*, it'll mean the school week finishes Thursday instead of Friday, so that according to House Rules I'll be allowed out that night. It means missing out on the weekend with Pug, but at least I'll see him fight, like I promised. I'll suggest it to Mum tomorrow morning while Dad's in the shower.

Done. All I've got to do is make up a date with Lisa and I'm out of here!

PS: Mum thought it was a great idea. I nearly laughed out loud as we schemed the whole thing out so that *Dad* would get maximum enjoyment from it all—when the whole idea is to get *me* a night out!

Mum gives the thumbs up as she comes into the kitchen in her nightshirt.

'It's on?' I say.

'Cat's Head Point, here we come. I'll ring up Maggie this morning and get her to give the house a once-over.'

'Oh, fab-oh!' I nearly tell her right then and there that I'm going out Thursday night (I'm so happy I'd like to tell her where, too, and who with!), but I keep control of myself.

'It was like pulling teeth, though.' Mum's back's to me as she starts making coffee.

'Yeah?' I pretend to care. Then I really do begin to wonder.

'What's wrong with that guy these days? He's off with the fairies half the time.'

'He is a bit . . . dreamy.' She stares at the coffee-maker, the scoop in her hand. At the back her hair is a little bit scrunched up from sleep, where she hasn't yet combed it. If you couldn't see those bony elbows you'd think it was a little kid standing there.

'He needs a holiday. Get him into the surf and he'll wake up a bit.'

'Yes.' The scoop dips into the coffee tin. 'It's always worked before. Coffee?'

Boy, will I be glad to get away from school early, next week. Brenner, every chance he can, *bumps* past me and hisses, 'Slut!' Sometimes he'll even call it out if he's with a bunch of friends. Ambra Lewis never meets my eyes, or if she does quickly glances away again. Josh sends me glances that say, *You? You are dirt. You are scum.* Lisa and Donna—well, there haven't been any condoms lately, but there are notes, regular notes, stuck on the back of my jumper for Mum to point out when I get home, turning up in my bag, scribbled on the first page in my folder, thrown from nowhere behind the teacher's back. I don't bother reading them any more.

I don't understand how they can think I'm any worse than them. I *know* I'm not. I used to be one of them. They're all having it off with each other, they're all getting as much sex as they can. I've been with them to those parties, bodies in every corner, everyone off their faces, the music like a screen over it all, so loud you can't talk, just *do*.

And I never did with anyone but Brenner—I never swapped and changed like some of them. If we're looking for sluts, the guys are the worst sluts, if half the stories they tell are true, of their endurance, repeat performances, girls and women they've 'had' (as if it were a con as well as a conquest). I was never quite sure what to do when those stories were doing the rounds—smile,

56

laugh? I'm sitting here with my boyfriend's arm around me while he says, of someone else, 'Yep. Had her. Up against a wall behind the fish shop,' and I'm supposed to *laugh*? I'm supposed to say, '*Fish* shop, that's a good one,' to show what a good sport I am? I'm supposed to ignore *hating* him, ignore wondering, *When was this? Did he catch anything from her that I should watch out for?*, ignore being incensed on this girl's behalf, for her being made into a piece of flesh that a guy *has* so that he can tell *these* guys he's had it? These people he's dying to impress, these fantastic role models? Beside these guys, and some of the girls, I'm a saint—faithful, loyal, tame.

I give up. This is just the lightning-strike of someone's boredom, someone's whim. (Donna's, probably; Lisa hasn't got enough imagination, and she wouldn't keep up the pressure for so long. She'll enjoy it while it lasts, but she hasn't got Donna's ill will towards everything, Donna's hatred and complete lack of a sense of humour.) I only have to wait, and react as little as possible, and eventually the boredom will seek another target. That, or the group will come up with some kind of grand finale to break me down, some way of signing off. I see myself lying in the schoolyard, hunks of hair ripped from my head, the marks of rocks and half-bricks on my legs and arms, my eyes closed, my stillness. Melanie Dow, martyr, Patron Saint of Defection from the Group. Well . . . I wonder how far they *would* go, though?

That acne-splattered geek Bruce Denman sits near me at lunchtime. A bunch of people are watching from under the camphor laurel on the far side of the yard, though not when I look up. I keep on eating. He eats, too, but keeps *staring* over at me. I'm supposed to be intimidated, I guess.

Finally he chucks his lunchbag and can in the bin and stands over me. He's a stupid guy, a real blockhead, but also very, very big. 'Wesley says you'll do it for $20.' Brenner Wesley, that is.

I look up and up and up, and then I say in this really mild voice, 'Well, he'd know, wouldn't he?'

'Guess he would,' Bruce says uncertainly. 'So, will you?'

'With you, you mean?'

'Yeah,' he says, with a real *nonchalant* little *swagger.*

'Oh, *sure*, Bruce,' I exclaim. 'You'd better show me your money first, though.'

Can you believe it, he tugs the corner of a $20 note up out of his jeans pocket so I can see it?

I'm so cool. 'Okay. Good. Now show me what you've got,' I say.

'Huh?'

'Show me the goods, buster. I've got to check you over for diseases, haven't I? I'm not going to ruin my professional life just because of your herpes, or crabs, or whatever you might have.'

'Well, I will show you. In private, but.'

'No way. Right here, mate, or the deal's off.'

He stares, backs off. 'You're crackers,' he says. 'You're raving mad.'

'Oh no. *Brenner Wesley's* mad, and *you're* mad, and all the other *shitheads* in this school are mad, but not me. And you can take your $20—' Here's where I see Mr Toohey standing at the corner of the building '—and stick it in your fat hairy *ear*hole!'

Some Year 7 kids are staring. I throw my rubbish in the bin, then head inside. I don't know why until I get to the locker room and realise I'm getting out of that school.

But uh-oh, Mr Toohey's there at the door, watching me get my bag out, and the few books I keep pushed right to the back. I get ready to stand up to him the way I just did to Bruce.

But he says, 'You're having a hard time this year, aren't you, Melanie?'

Oh God, don't be understanding. Tell me off, give me an excuse to shout at you. 'I'm okay,' I say, my voice stiff, not looking at him.

'School counsellor?' he says tentatively.

'Oh, no.' I'm able to smile. 'Telling people things is what started it all off.'

'Counsellors have codes of practice. They have to keep things private, not like normal, free, individuals.' *Curse them*, he seems to be implying. It's funny, the way he isn't bothering to chat, to soften any of this. It's like an emergency bulletin, as if he hasn't got much time to get through to me. He's being nice, really. I glance at him as I shut my locker door and for the second before the tears arrive he looks like someone I might have talked to, if it wasn't already too late.

'Thanks. No.' Head down, I go past him. I bash the tears away before I get outside, and then I go across the yard with my head up. No-one calls out anything. I know Mr Toohey has come out after me and is watching. I also know he won't stop me.

I walk home. Dad's car is outside. *Here we go. He's finally cracked up from overwork and been sent home to recuperate.*

He's left the gate open, even though he always goes on at me to close it.

I put my key in the door.

From inside, Dad yells out, 'Don't come in!'

I come in.

There he is, *at it* on the couch with Ricky Lewis. Her little white shorts tossed aside on the carpet. One bare foot hooked on the couch back. That couch really isn't quite long enough; Dad's legs slew off to the floor. His white bum parked between Ricky's bent knees, his trousers halfway down. Beyond the shadow of his balls, parts of Ricky *glisten*, glistening down onto *our* couch. And the expression on her face (she's gaping at me over Dad's shoulder)—well, you wouldn't want to meet a person again after seeing them look like that. Mega-doses of guilt and fear! She hardly looks human.

All this I take in in half a second, closing the door behind me.

'Is she gone?' says Dad in a little peeping voice, muffled in a cushion.

'No,' gasps Ricky, still staring at me over the foot she's got in the middle of Dad's back. She's panting, and so's he, *from their exertions*. I'm breathing hard too; the room sounds like an aerobics class with the music turned off.

'Melanie, get out, *darling*,' says Ricky.

I should stay. I should sit down on the other couch and watch them pull apart, get their clothes together, cover up the horrible old *bits* they've been using, all in a big hurry, babbling explanations, or possibly in an awful silence. I *should*.

I run upstairs instead and sit in my room, my blood thundering. After a minute, Ricky knocks. 'Melanie?' She's still got that edge of threat in her voice, as if *I'm* the one in trouble. I say in a very *icy* voice, 'Get out of this house.'

I feel a fantastic explosion of virtue inside myself as I say it. *Nothing* I've *ever* done can be as bad, half as bad, as what Dad has done. No humiliation I've ever felt can be as devastating, as un-get-overable as what those two must be feeling. Beside these grown people and their gigantic mistake, I'm a mere apprentice, just *toying* with the edges of silliness, of harmfulness. So there's this joy that falls with the hammerblows of harm that cancel it out—a joyless joy, a hard, cold relief.

'You have to under*stand*, Melanie—'

'Come on, Rick,' Dad says at the foot of the stairs. 'I'll drop you off home.' He must know it'll be hopeless talking to me.

You have to understand! Boy, do I understand! All of a sudden quite a few things are a whole lot clearer. I go over and over Dad's behaviour, and Ricky's for the last few months, watching it all fall into place—her dropping by, Dad staying out late, Mum wondering what the fuck's going on with him. Mum! God! How can I tell her? How can I not? When I think of Mum, that's when I have to get up and leave, get out of that house, that 'family home'. I'm running down the stair carpet I helped them choose; past the couch we got last year (we all sat in a row on it when it arrived, smiling self-satisfaction); past the phone table Mum sanded back and rubbed endless layers of shellac onto (I remember her serious face as she stood there looking at it, not wanting to admit it was finished, restored).

I'm nearly frantic by the time I get to Pug's. I knock and knock, but no-one answers, and I'm just about to sit down and start crying when I realise it's training time. I fly across Erskine-ville Road to the Club, hurry upstairs. It's like stepping inside someone's body—all the blows thudding around me like a pulse, and the wet, wet heat on my face.

Pug, oh Pug. You're there, a shining body fitting the gap in front of my eyes. You don't see me—I'm a fly on the wall. You look so serious I cross the room in my mind, dodging Justin at the bag and two other guys skipping rope. I swear I feel my arms slither right around you from over by the wall—I'm loving every-thing of you right down to the way you sniff, showing your top teeth in a dog-snarl. I needed to see you so *badly*, and now I sit just inside the door, and let myself fill right up with you. You push the day and the afternoon, that whole other life, right out of my head.

☻☻. I don't tell Pug anything. I'm just with him, silent, recovering.

Okay. Now I won't see him until he steps out into the ring on Thursday night. Flutter, flutter. As if I didn't have enough to panic about.

Normal life, the gruesome things it can hide. If Mum would only give her frustrated cry, 'What is *wrong* with you two?' I could point, I could say, 'What is wrong is, *he* . . .' But she doesn't. She's chirpily preparing for our weekend away. She's so happy and lively it seems like she knows everything and is putting on a monstrous pretence of not knowing.

I haven't even seen Dad in the two days since. Working late, the bastard. I hear him come in and shower, knowing the reason for all those showers now. Because nothing's been said, I look back to Monday afternoon and wonder if it really did happen. Maybe I dreamed it, my brain hunting out someone else to blame for my troubles.

Mum looks up from her list-making. 'It'll be a big shop, Thursday night.'

'Oh, I can't come. I promised Lees I'd go out with her.'

'Oh, rats. I finally coaxed Dad into coming.'

'Good, you won't be on your own, then.'

'I thought Lisa wasn't allowed out week-nights either.'

'They bent the rules, 'cause I'm going to be away.'

'Oh, well.' She glances down her list. 'Dad and I'll just have to have an intimate candlelit dinner for two. Shucks, eh?'

I manage a sickly smile.

I'm at the Club. Oriana's nails dig into my elbow, the crowd of mostly men and feral children stamps, claps and calls 'Di-no! Di-no! Di-no!' as his team escorts him down the aisle from the dressing room. Over the raised ring, small, bare, spotlit, hang two white cards:

DINO MAGNINI	MAGNUM POULOS
Weight 71.1 kg	Weight 76.3 kg
	8 × 2 mins

Magnum Poulos is already in the ring, shedding a long crimson satin robe and a white T-shirt. He's big and dark and tough-looking, with a black frizz of hair bursting off the top of his head. 'Oh God, I hate him already,' says Oriana in my ear.

Pug, robed in hot red, looks magnificent, a warrior king coming down through his battalions. He's a different creature from the restless, speechless person in the dressing-room, needing us there but blind and deaf to everything but Jimmy's reassurances. Now he seeks us out in the crowd before climbing up into the ring. *Right, on with the business.* I'm *appalled* at what's about to happen (can this be the twentieth century?), at what I've got myself into, caring for someone who subjects himself to this. I glance at Mrs Magnini, who sits with her handbag on her lap, her eyes on the ring. It must be ten times worse for her. The others, Pug's dad and Oriana and Luciano, are going mental like the rest of the crowd, cheering madly.

You can see those extra five kilos on Magnum Poulos; he's a bit bigger all over. Pug looks unperturbed, stripped down to hot red shorts, testing the surface of the ring. Can this be the same guy, mine, the man in the green-shadowed room in the long summer afternoons? He looks horribly alone up there, despite the whistles and the crowd calling out, despite his team and the officials encrusting the edges of the ring.

Jimmy Riley ties a pair of bright red gloves onto him. The guy with the megaphone introduces them and the crowd cheers for Poulos and goes bananas for Pug. Then the ref has his little mutter to them (what does he say? A little prayer? 'Follow Plan B tonight, lads—it's Magnum's turn to win'?), and they go to their corners and wait for the bell. *Oh God, I don't want to see this. Is there a way to stop time?* Clanng! *No, there isn't.*

They go straight after each other like sworn enemies, no dancing, no hanging back. Pug is up against the ropes in a few seconds, but he slips out and around and traps Magnum in a corner. Then too much is going on for me to follow; they're locked together and trying to punch upward between each other's fists. This is so different from training; there's no Jimmy calling the shots, there's no imaginary opponent. Instead, a big angry body is trying to pound Pug into oblivion.

I can't believe the crowd. As soon as the fight starts the ones up the front are all shouting advice ('Body-body-body, Dino!', 'Work 'im, Magnum, work 'im! Don't let 'im rest!', 'And again, Dino! Body again!'), which is loud enough, but when either of the fighters gets a scoring blow in there's this—it isn't a roar and it isn't a cheer—it's a big *rush* of male voice noise. A roar of joy? And then the advice goes up to a new pitch, and after the next blow and rush of noise, an even higher, louder one. Guys are practically climbing into the seat in front of them, their faces red and yelling, veins popping out in their necks—their eyes focused

63

without blinking on the ring. It's absolutely one of the weirdest things I've ever seen, heard or experienced.

I never thought two minutes could last so long. When the bell goes I'm really ready for a break.

Oriana stops screaming and sits down. 'How do you like it?'

'It sucks,' I say, my eyes on Pug. He's aglow with sweat on a stool in his corner, Jimmy talking in his ear.

'Don't faint, willya?' Oriana grins. She looks up at the ring, turns her head away sharply. 'Now *this* bit sucks.'

A little *doll* of a girl, dressed in a tight, tight, sequined, very short mini dress, comes tottering up to the ring on spiky heels. When she bends down to climb through the ropes whistles and shouts explode all over the hall because one half of the crowd can see down her front and the other half can see up her backside.

'What's she doing?' I ask Oriana. Neither fighter takes a scrap of notice of her.

She stands up and smirks her way around the ring, holding up the round number written on a little card. The feral kids whistle and clap. Some man in the crowd yells encouragement, and she pauses and lifts her skirt so he can see her sequined knickers—she gets lots of applause for this.

What the— 'Does that happen every round?'

'Different bird every time,' says Oriana. 'It's off, isn't it?'

But the bell's gone and everyone's melted off the ring except for Pug and Magnum and the referee.

They're a perfect match; for every good blow he puts in, Pug gets one in return. He takes a couple of smacking body blows and the crowd *howls*, echoing the little howl of fear in my innards. But he pushes forward straight away, and lands a really solid blow to the side of Magnum's head. Magnum doesn't even stagger; his head pops up and he comes in close and locks it into Pug's shoulder. It looks weird, almost affectionate.

The referee has to tell them to break quite a few times this round, and the boxing seems messy, with Pug basically fending off the other guy and not getting any openings. When the bell goes he swings away to his corner. Both guys are glossy and beginning to drip, with red patches where they've been hit, and Magnum's black frizz is draggling onto his shiny forehead. He still looks massive, and angry now, dangerous.

The Round 3 girl, in a gold-beaded bikini, trips past him, delicate as an insect, cheerfully flashing a breast at one of her supporters. 'Oh, gross,' says Oriana, turning away. Beside her Luciano is watching the girl and grinning.

'Onyer, Dino! Don't wait for 'im!' someone yells when the bell goes for the third round. Magnum locks Pug into that embrace again and forces him back towards his corner. Pug shakes himself free. He steps back and sideways and puts four neat, hard blows into Magnum's ear and jaw. Half the crowd hollers with outrage and the other half hollers with joy. Oriana and Lu are jumping in their places. Magnum turns and tries to push in on Pug again, but through his elbows Pug slips a blow to his chest. He gets hit on the forehead for that, but comes back so quickly that Magnum's up against the corner pad, taking a bunch of blows full in his face before he butts his way out. Pug's face over Magnum's charging back has no emotion on it at all; then it disappears; it reappears red where their foreheads have connected and the brow-bones have squashed the flesh apart, and there's still no emotion—no shock, no pain, nothing. The crowd is no longer voices, but a surging sea of noises, Oriana's screams lost in it. Mrs Magnini leans against me, craning for a view, hanging onto my arm. Pug's dad is on his feet and yelling with the rest. Pug ducks a swipe before the referee stops the fight and makes him check with the doctor.

He's allowed to continue. The next time they come together Magnum falls to one knee on the canvas and is counted out to three. He stands up and goes forward. Pug pushes him back onto the ropes and gives him three big, *meaty* punches in the head, right-left-right, yanking three *great* big roars out of the crowd. I go into shock. *This is a person's head, not a sawdust-stuffed bag. So this is what is meant by 'a decisive victory' in boxing.*

Magnum's fists sag away from his face. The referee stops the fight again, has a very short exchange with Magnum, then turns and gives the match to Pug.

'That's it?' I say to Oriana.

'Yes, yes!' She flings an arm around me and jumps about cheering wildly.

Pug's mum squeezes my hand, then lets go to hunt for a hankie in her bag.

The two fighters look as if they've been shovelling coal in a furnace all day: the sweat splashes off them, their fancy shorts are dull and soaked. Pug lifts his arms like a bear, and then seems to notice the crowd for the first time as it roars all round him.

He turns full circle to acknowledge all the applause. He doesn't smile at all, as if he's just taking what's due to him, no big deal. And then he's looking at me, standing still and meeting my eyes down a *tunnel* in the most incredible, inhuman racket. Buildings fall, mountains crumble all around, but *inside* the tunnel is absolute silence. He could whisper and I would hear every word, I swear. His eyes snap wide awake then, and there's a half-smile on his mouth, a really *ironic* one, when I just didn't think Pug was an ironic type of person, didn't think he had that level of thinking in him. It's as if he knows everything I've been thinking about this crazy sport, and he thinks it all too, but then there's *this* on top of it, the winning. He can still put himself up there, risk his face and his brain, for this. It means something. *Can you see what it means to me, Mel?* No, I can't. I can see that it *does* matter, but I don't think I'll ever know why.

Then the tunnel blinks out, and the racket makes me jump, like a bang of thunder. He turns away to accept a hug from Magnum and Jimmy and his team. A shining rain begins to fall; people are throwing handfuls of coins. The money rings in the air overhead and splashes onto the canvas.

Pug is whisked away, a thick knot of people hugging him and

66

shaking his hand and slapping his back as Jimmy leads him up the aisle.

I feel as if I haven't breathed since the match started. Dazed, I follow the Magninis through to the change-room, grateful for the crowd that slows us, holds me upright, gives me a chance to recover.

I trail in with the family, stand by while they all embrace and congratulate and cry on him. It feels as if hardly a minute's passed since we were all in here watching Pug psych himself up. Now we're all different people. He won, and we saw him do it.

Over his dad's shoulder he sees me. Come on over, he gestures with his head, his taped hand. I wangle my way through, feeling awestruck, tiny as a round-card girl.

'Outa me way, Dad,' he says, pretending to push him aside. And here is my Pug—non-ironic, bloodied and beautiful, kissing me with a grunt of emphasis, grinning a sparkling grin at me under the split eyebrow, lifting me off my feet and swinging me round. I bury my face in his neck, in that ridiculous red robe, so no-one will see my tears.

'So, what d'you think of me new job?' he says, putting me down.

'I don't know,' I say shakily. 'I think I hate it.'

He laughs, and Magninis laugh around me. Someone pats me on the back, as if to say, *You'll come round to it.*

But I don't believe I ever can, ever will, be anything but puzzled. Puzzled, and frightened.

'Siddown, Dino, and let me finish with that cut,' says Jimmy.

We all sit around while Jimmy swabs and Oriana, Lu and Mr Magnini do a post-mortem of the fight. Mrs Magnini sits beaming, dabbing at her eyes now and then. And every now and again you look at me, you pug, you Pug, and I have to stop myself saying it, out loud and in front of everyone (God, wouldn't we all be embarrassed!), because of your green eyes, your hand trailing tape, your damp-patched T-shirt and the black hair curling along your legs, because of the mist of victory-glamour between us, and your same old rusty voice assenting, describing, enthusing in Italian. But as far as I know how to love anybody I love you, whatever it means. I don't know how someone like you can be a fighter for a living, or how such fighting can be fair, within the rules, but I'll claim the privilege, I'll sit in the post-victory dressing-room with you, any time!

And of course, ⊕☉. Feels like a star-fuck, except that he seems to think *I'm* the star.

'Felt so good when I saw you come in, up the Club,' he says afterwards. 'Knew I'd win then. Couldn't let you see me lose, first fight you ever seen, eh.'

'Would've put me right off.'

'Me too. You wanna get to the top without losing at all, if you can. You know, "undefeated in 32 matches, 24 by knockout". You read about it in *The Fist* like that all the time.'

I let my jaw drop.

'What's up?'

'*I* didn't realise you could *read*!'

He looks taken aback. 'Course I can bloody *read*! What d'you reckon I do with all these?' He waves his arm around, obviously meaning the magazines rather than the socks.

I can't stop myself cracking up. 'I thought you just looked at the *p-pictures*!' But he's caught on—he's gripping me tight in his arms and legs. 'Aagh, aagh! Help! I'm being suffoca—' I run out of breath from laughing.

His nose is in my ear. At the edge of my sight I can see the tiny bandaids holding his eyebrow together. 'Sometimes,' he says, half-serious, half-laughing, 'You're a bitch and a cow. You know that?'

He keeps giving me, hard, suffocating squeezes. 'I kno-*ho*. A ba-*hitch* anna ca-*how*.' Splutter, splutter. 'But not all the ti-*hime*!' I rush in before the next squeeze.

'Nah, not all the time,' he agrees, relaxing a bit but still holding pretty tight. 'Hardly ever. You're all right.'

'I'll do, will I?' I try to turn and look at him but his head's in the way.

He puts his hand up to my other cheek and holds on. 'Yeah,' he *growls*.

And, of course, ⊕⊖ again.

Well, here we are at the cottage, all together as a family. Isn't that *sweet*? Isn't that *lovely*? Except every time I see you diving into a wave, Dad, I can't help remembering you diving into old Rick.

It's amazing how hard it is to believe it happened now. The way Dad's acting you'd think everything was fine. I've kept away from situations where I might be left alone with him, just in case he starts talking about it. No, *thanks*; no explanations, *please*! 'Your mother doesn't understand me, Mel' or, 'A man's got to feel he's attractive, Mel' or, 'You mustn't be too hard on Ricky, Mel. She's a lonely woman.' Or some other crap.

And Mum's quite normal, of course, even though half the time I'm screaming at her (in my brain) about what I saw and what a bastard Dad is. She's in holiday mode—so peaceful, so determined to see the bright side of things. Maybe Dad's been porking everything that *moves*, with her *consent*, for *years*, while she refuses to make a fuss *to hold the family together*. Maybe she knows all about Ricky—but if she *doesn't*, I can't exactly go up to her and say 'Do you *know* Dad's having it off with one of your best friends?', can I?

Do you know, Mum?

If I don't stop the thoughts they build and build until they gridlock in my brain and I'm shaking with rage and powerlessness. Thoughts of Mum and Ricky, laughing and laughing—Ricky on that couch and Mum on the floor, unable to stop. Ricky. Ricky being everywhere we looked, the last few months. At home with Dad a couple of times when we got back after the shopping. (Well, no wonder he didn't want to come with us—he'd miss his regular Thursday-night gig with Rick, wouldn't he?) Dropping by. Borrowing things so she'd have an excuse to bring them back.

Still doing all the things they usually do—tennis Wednesdays, all four of them; Sunday morning coffee just her and Mum, over at Leichhardt. Ricky standing at our kitchen door, all legs and nipples. 'Don't mind if I do,' she says to Dad. And him all rumpled, busily getting out glasses! Busily covering up!

Ambra, glaring. Joshua, spitting. I go cold. How long's it been going on? Have Josh and Ambra seen what I've seen? Worse? What are we all going to do?

Sitting here in my room in the beach house with Mum and Dad out on the deck reading the newspapers, oh so civilised, is sending me mad, not knowing what to think or do. When my brain wears itself out playing the Dad-and-Ricky video and the fight video, I go out and exercise my legs instead, walk the bay beach to the rocks and watch the grey water going wild, stride the never-ending surf beach with the sea-thunder coming up through the sand, rinse my head out with wind and water and space until there's not a single thought-scrap left. I'm trying to give Mum and Dad time to get back together properly—you know, you guys,⊕☉! Do it! 'Rediscover each other', like the magazines suggest, revive your jaded marriage! Isn't that kind of me? I'm so considerate! When I'm there watching the way they're together-without-being-together it seems crazy to hope, but who knows what goes on when I leave? One look from Dad to Mum, one recognition ('How could I do this to her?' or, 'She's still the Jan I married, really—why didn't I see that?') and the situation—his, mine, Ricky's, this terrible hovering—might begin to fix itself up.

Went shopping with Mum this morning, for a few last things for the party. Ooh boy, am I looking forward to this party! Aren't you, Dad? Aren't you *itching* to sit at the dinner table and look around at the happy, birthday-candle-lit faces of your loving family, Mum so innocent, me so *knowing*?! Don't be scared, Dad, I won't say anything—not yet, anyway. I mean, I *could* do a Lisa and use that knowing to get myself a car for my seventeenth, or an all-expenses-paid trip overseas or something. But things are

70

bad enough already. This whole weekend feels like a sick joke I'm playing, a joke on myself as much as on those two. I got to see the fight, but now I face the payoff, *exile* with my estranged parents.

You've obviously settled on keeping your head down, Dad, hoping it'll all go away. I've read that that's what unfaithful men do. I mean, Ricky's probably been pleading with you to leave us (though I don't think *her* kids are all that impressed with you) and you've probably promised her you will 'when the time's right'—and the time'll never be right, right? It's just too *comfortable* where you are, and too *interesting* and *exciting* stringing two women along. Yours and Mum's sex life is probably sparking up nicely, you being all sexed up from your affair—like, if I whipped home now I might find you and her, similar scenario but a different pair of legs wrapped round you, you with your eyes shut tight imagining the other one.

Aagh, it's *disgusting*, and you *know* it is, Dad, and I'd like to see you *admitting* it. You'll have to at some stage, I know that much—you aren't going to just cruise through this and tell me on your death-bed, 'Well, we had our ups and downs, Mel, but you know I always loved your mother and at least we *kept the family together*.' And that's such an achievement, isn't it? Physical proximity is all you'd be talking about. Sure, we were a *close* family, always in each other's pockets. We never talked, never knew what was on each other's minds, but heck, there we were, all *together*, no-one could deny it.

So what do you say, Dad? Will I tell Mum right there over the roast lamb and spuds tomorrow night—your favourite meal, forever tainted by the memory? I could just drink a *little* bit too much champagne, and the words I've been bottling up for six days would come tumbling out while Mum looked at me and then at you, her eyes getting wider and wider, that contented smile draining away from her face.

What would she do? Spit on you? Scream? Run down the hill and plunge into the freezing surf? She'd probably do something really boring like go to the bedroom and close the door. Then I'd go for a walk and when I came back you'd have *sorted it all out*, told her a bunch of lies to keep her calm, and things would go back to *normal*. Nice for you—I couldn't hack it though, Dad. When your brain's been stretched with a new idea, they reckon, it can never go back to the size it was. Now that I've seen you adulter-ing I can hardly see any of you that *isn't* the adulterer. A big question mark hovers over all the rest—how could you have been a *loving father* or a *loyal husband* one day, and a bastard the next? There must have been the seeds of bastardry there all the time.

Having seen what I saw . . . The impossibility of undoing events, the fact that I can't perform a fast-reverse—just a few seconds would be enough—so I didn't hear that room with its cross-currents of panting, didn't see . . . that. Detail after undignified detail, clear as clear. I blush for you and Ricky, Dad, it feels like all the time. I think it's really strange—it makes it worse, somehow—that you can continue to walk upright, pretend nothing's happened. You're so good at it—so *practised*?, I can't help thinking. I flip through our family life like a secret photo album, dreadful new pictures popping up on each page.

My only comfort is Pug. I feel as if he's saved my life. Not just before, putting his protective layers between me and school, between me and my 'friends', but now, even in this dire place, giving me a whole other area of life to escape to. I can imagine really clearly what he'd be doing now, absorbed in training, and then coming home, showering, throwing on crumpled clothes and leaving for his parents' place to 'sort 'em out', or up to King Street to hang out with his mates. He'd be missing me but he'd never say anything to anyone about it—just like me. Private. Keep Out.

'I appreciate you being discreet about this, Mel,' you say in the two accidental seconds we get together in the car. Our eyes meet in the mirror.

'Covering for you, do you mean?' I sneer. 'Is that what you think I'm doing?'

'Whatever you're doing'—you can see Mum heading back to the car—'it's right not to hurt Mum.'

I could strangle you, you horrible blackmailing *philanderer*. If Mum wasn't coming back I'd scream at you, but instead I say sweetly, 'Oh, you're so right. After all, it's nothing to do with *her*, is it?'

Mum's bum hits the passenger seat. 'To do with whom?'

'Lisa.' I glance away from Dad's eyes in the mirror. 'I hate her.'

'I thought you were best friends. What's she done now?'

So I have to make up a ridiculous story about this *tiff* Lisa and I are having—not a serious enough one for us to split *permanently*, because she's such a useful 'best friend' to have—how would I ever get to see Pug without my 'dates' with Lisa?

So anyway, you're off the hook—for the moment, Dad, for the moment only, so don't get too comfortable. *Being discreet*—gee, you make me sick! 'It's right not to hurt *Mum*'—you were thinking of *Mum's* happiness all the time Ricky was *raping* you, right? You were weeping with sympathy for *Mum*. Calling her 'Mum' was a good ploy. *Remember, Mel, you have a duty not to hurt your mum, after all she's done for you.* Well, you can keep your Ricky-sticky paws off Mum and me; it's *your* leg of the tripod that's looking shaky. Just because I'm keeping quiet now doesn't mean I'll be quiet for ever. Sometime when I can't stand all the pretending any longer I'm going to tell her—I *am*! I'm not going to *be discreet* about it, either—I'm going to shout it out good and loud, possibly even up and down our street: 'David Dow screws around! I know! I saw him screwing Ricky Lewis in our front room! Third of April, one-thirty p.m.!' And old Mr Close'll lean over his balcony railing and sing out, 'Think we don't know, young Melanie? Think we haven't sat here all day and seen him

73

popping in and out with every woman in the neighbourhood?' Well, Dad, how do I know you *haven't*, now that I know you *could*?

Dad led me down to the water. His hand wrapped mine halfway to the elbow; I was the height of the bottom edge of his bathers. The waves ran at me, eye-high, hurried, their tops juggling froth. At the last moment he swung me up so that the ocean only dashed the sand from my feet, leaving them fizzing cold.

Our beach weekend recedes, just one small bracket of a long-running nightmare. It gets colder, and wetter, and darker—and quieter in our house. It's as if we're all going into hibernation, just gradually shutting down. Our mouths don't talk much, so we don't have to use our ears much (though Mum sometimes puts music on, 'to cheer us up'—huh!). And of course we can't meet each other's eyes any more so soon our sight will go. Then we'll just all lie down on our beds and fade away for six months, and when the spring comes we'll wake up being new people, with different lives, and all the crappy stuff from *these* lives forgotten, swept away with six months' worth of dreams, just another uncomfortable dream.

I'm getting so used to living in unbearable tension, if it all went away I think my teeth'd fly out of their sockets from not being clenched. 'It's a difficult year,' say the teachers—if they just *knew* how difficult!

Donna and Lisa come in the school gate behind me. I hear their scheming silence even before I look.

'We're gunna *strip* you, Dow,' says Donna.

I'm sick of this. I turn around and stop. 'Yeah? What for?'

They glance at each other. 'What do you reckon?' Donna says contemptuously.

'Yeah, Mel. Jesus!' adds Lisa.

'Beats me.'

'Hey, that's a good idea. Strip her and then bash her up. Leave her in a gutter somewhere.'

'Yeah. Where she *belongs*.' Lisa slides past me after Donna and they go off laughing.

I drift up from sleep one stolen Thursday afternoon to find Pug looking into my face. 'What?' I say.

'Is anythink wrong, Mel?'

Long pause. 'Every-bloody-thing's wrong.' Just saying that much, the rush of relief is *huge*!

'Shit, what'd I do?' Talk about look terrified! I have to laugh.

'Not you, you idiot!'

He puts his hand on his heart to calm it down. 'Who is it, then? Who's giving you the shits?'

'My parents. My dad, specifically. *Everyone* at school, except maybe one teacher—'

'Hang on. What's your dad goin' on about, first?'

I tell him about finding Dad and Ricky together. I watch him all through it, to get his exact reaction.

A couple of times he winces as if he's about to stop me speaking. He punctuates my story with little moans of distress.

'Jesus, I thought my family had problems!' he says when I finish. He swears a few more times, absorbing it. 'What'll your mum do when she finds out?'

'*If* she finds out.'

'Y'gunna tell 'er?'

'Sometime. I'm not sure when.'

'I reckon you should. She should know, don't you think? I mean, you can't let someone go on not knowing . . . somethin' like that, eh.'

'Eh.' I look into his clean green worried eyes. 'Yeah, you're right, I guess. Any day now I will. Any old day.' He still looks worried. 'I will, I will.'

'That's bad news, mate.' *Mate*. I love that. He means it in a companionable kind of way, but also it's *my mate*, the way birds choose a mate.

'You're telling me.' Having him know, having anyone else know (well, I guess Josh and Ambra know and that's no comfort)—having Pug know and be on my side, and hearing his concern, which is my concern but minus my anger, clears my mind. It's not just pure outrage in there any more, revolving on itself, dizzying me into inaction; I can see through that to the massive changes that hang on my telling Mum. It's still up to me to make the move, to tip the truth into Mum's brain and watch her world, and Dad's, and mine, go to pieces, or at least shudder on its axis for a while. Pug has just shown me, with his ducking and wincing, what a cup of poison I'm holding; he's never even met these people and he can feel the pain.

'What about school? What's happenin' there?'

'The usual hassles.' *Slut. Thinks she's too good to talk to anyone any more. Stackin' on the weight, aren't you?* All that crap. 'There's no-one there I get on with.'

'That bloke you told me about, is he still giving y'a hard time?'

'Oh yeah, that too.' A pathetic little laugh comes out of me. 'Feel like I'm down the bottom of a black hole with slippery sides, and just can't get out. *Nothing's* any good at the moment.'

He sits up and pulls me over so I'm lying in his arms like a baby. '*We're* okay, aren't we? I'm not gettin' up your nose, am I?'

'I don't think you could get up my nose if you tried.'

'I wouldn't *wanna* try.' He pulls the blankets closer round me, rocks me, pushes back my hair. His face is very light and happy—any minute I expect him to start humming a tune.

'You're really nice, you know?' I say. 'If I didn't have you to come round and see, I'd've shot myself by now.'

'Nah, you wouldn't cop out like that.'

'Wouldn't I?' I'm surprised—he sounds so sure.

'Nah, you're too smart. You wouldn't let a bunch of dickhead schoolkids get to you that bad.'

'No? Seems to me I've been doing just that for six months or so already.'

'You're workin' on other stuff, but. In your head. I hear you, the way you talk. The minute you get out of the place . . . and it's only six or seven months now, hey? Hang on—May, June—' He counts on his fingers. 'Yeah, six months, and there's holidays in there too, remember. Six months, and then you can kiss 'em all off.'

'And do what?'

'I dunno. Whatever you make up your mind to. You're like a firecracker someone's lit. It's goin' along that stringy bit—'

'The fuse.'

'Yeah, and right now you're just spittin' and sparkin' and shit, but when you get to the end, when you hit the powder . . .'

'Everybody stand back, hey?'

'Everyone stand back, because you're gunna blow *right* over our heads! You're gunna be *way* up there!'

'You're going to be there to see it, are you?'

Oh Pug, the look on your face! I could *kick* myself! Sort of I-guess-not, sort of I-hope-so—and you hesitate, when before you were in full flight.

'If I'm lucky,' you say very quietly.

'Well, so far you've been pretty lucky.' I try to make up for putting my great fat foot in it.

'Yeah, so far.'

You don't sound all that convinced, so I reach up and pull your head down, and you lift mine up in the crook of your elbow, and we kiss in the middle. After that we're all right.

Surrounded by the placenta, the twelve-week-old foetus inhales salty amniotic fluid, but draws its oxygen from the blood supplied by the umbilical cord. It now contains its full complement of operational body systems. Nerves, muscles and the developing permanent skeleton are readying the arms and legs for their first movements. True bone is forming rapidly, displacing the cartilage of the embryonic skeleton, which acts as a mould for the stiff calcium layers. In the long arm and leg bones, the calcium is first laid down in the middle of the bones, progressing outwards in both directions. The body wall, beginning at the spine, has grown forward and is now joined at the front.

I walk home through the falling evening. A period must come soon. It weighs low in me, solid like a lodged apple. The blood is well and truly gathered and ready. *Tonight*. The ache is big enough, and I feel faintly feverish, and all those tears . . . all the signs point to it.

Mum's cooking up some Italian thing when I get home, all garlic and tomatoes. Just the sight of the olive-oil bottle makes me back out the kitchen door, without having spoken to her. Up in my room I listen to the hormones chug and feel myself turning into a pre-menstrual monster. Pug looks crazy, cradling me and telling me fireworks stories. Why is he stupidly not seeing this black me, wimping out on life at every turn, letting herself be victimised, fucked over, dragged around by anyone who offers her the first scrap of approval? So I've fooled him—these others aren't fooled, these parents who're so tired and impatient with me all the time, these schoolkids who've seen how easy I am. They all know the worst.

Night comes, and I don't turn the light on. Mum comes up when tea's ready. 'Oh dear,' she says when she sees me curled on the bed. 'That time again, is it?'

She leaves me in the dark, in the dread, in a place where nobody can make me feel any better. Bodies do this to you. It's just a matter of electricity in your brain: suddenly all the switches are down and the black chemicals flood in among your thoughts, staining them all, blotting out the bright ones.

In the middle of the night I wake up boiling in my clothes, shed some layers, crawl under the covers, drag sleep back over me.

In the morning I wake clean and dry, not bleeding. 'This is getting ridiculous,' I say out loud, for courage.

Home pregnancy tests come in packets of two. They are reliable, the girl at the chemist said; if they are faulty they'll tell you you're not pregnant when you are, not the other way around. In four minutes I am standing in the bathroom with the test in my hand, the thin blue line in the tester window as clear as it can be. There's no denying it, no possibility of a mistake.

There was a bleed with the miscarriage. There was another, when, January? Sometime. There may've been two. It must be three, four months. It must be—

I dig my fingers into my belly. Yesterday's apple, still there. Quite firm. Not about to be bled away.

In the mirror my face is the same old face I've dragged through every crisis. I am one of those pale people, English-pale, always sunscreened to within an inch of my life. My hair is a mess of black squiggles escaping from their band. There are pillowcase-crease marks up one cheek like a very old person's wrinkles.

The house is so quiet. Mum and Dad's alarm hasn't gone off yet. Thank God. I hurry out, dress. I write a note to Mum, two hard truths, numbered (a) and (b). I push it, in an envelope marked, 'Mum', under their bedroom door. I run. I am a coward. I flee. I slam out the door. I hurry up our street, which is foreign, autumn fresh. Mr Close, walking Nelson the bull-terrier, greets me kindly; I bare my teeth at him in an approximation of a smile. I'm past, I'm gone—except that your self always follows you. I'm hurrying, breaking into a run, wanting to be lost in traffic, the world to swallow me up.

Crossing the park I realise I'm going blind. A patch of blindness has started at the centre of my right eye and is growing. I know what this is: a migraine. Mum's told me about them. The blindness spreads; I have to peer around it to see the right-hand side of the path. I stand on the kerb at King Street, my head darting like a chook's so that I can see what I need to see with my left eye. I check twice that the light is green before I cross.

Two small catherine wheels are whirling at the left-hand fringe of my vision. As I turn into Pug's street they are raining fire into my left cheek. My other eye is blank, dead. By the time Pug opens the door I can only recognise him by his voice. There is a short nightmare of huge stairs and runaway limbs. Then there is a bed—it could be on a wall or the ceiling for all I can tell—and Pug sounding soothing somewhere and his hand keeping me from toppling into a swamp of nausea. I can't speak or see out of my body.

We wait it out. Things steady slightly; the nausea fades. Sight begins where it first disappeared, a pinpoint in my right eye, gradually clearing.

'This is a migraine,' I'm finally able to say. 'My mum gets them. They hit your eyes first, and then they wallop you on the head.' *How did I get here?*

Pug's head is radiant, four-dimensional with beauty, a great leaning statue-with-feeling, a memorial for every young soldier ever slaughtered. 'You be okay while I go get some Panadol?'

'I'm fine now.'

He lets go, and I lounge about two centimetres above the bed like a slightly drunken flying carpet. Immense well-being furs my body from hair-ends to toe-tips. *Perhaps this will get rid of the baby.*

Then I hear the distant hunting-horns of the headache, almost pleasant, negligible. Pug comes back with a glass of fizzing medicine-water. I sit up and drink it under the first hoofbeats.

'I told Mum, about Dad. I left a note. I had to get away from there,' I explain. Any minute now I'll go on and explain the rest.

'A note? Christ.'

'What?'

'That's hard. Terrible way to find out. Hard to write, too.'

'I just put the bald truth.' *Truths, Mel. Two of them, remember?*

'Jesus, your poor mum.'

'I couldn't go on covering up for him—' But I'm beginning to wish I were blind again. The light gallops in, over the hedges and ridges of my brain. This will definitely do the baby in; if it feels half this pain it will not want to be borne, to be born. I curl up like a foetus myself, or like a slater, or a snail's eye retreating into its stalk. Where did that drug go, sopped up into the blood-thunder? I need more. Knock me out. I curl up smaller.

I lose track of time. If you lie still with your hands over your eyes, sooner or later you'll fall asleep, and when I finally achieve sleep it's the coma type, a complete disappearance.

When I wake up I'm flat on my back like a corpse, the head-ache pooled in the back of my skull like a teaspoonful of ink. Eventually I open my eyes. Pug's gone. Afternoon, quite late. He must be at training. I don't miss him. I don't miss anyone. I'm grateful for this empty room. This morning's events filter through to me, seriously horrifying.

Maybe Dad picked up the letter, realised what it must be, hid it from Mum. Maybe everything is still as it was. No, Mum always gets up first. Dad's nearest the door, though. Surely he'd sense me behind it, hear that rub of paper on the carpet, leap awake to rescue himself? Or would he lie there, like me now, while Mum tied her dressing-gown and bent—'What's this?'—and laid hold of the envelope, while she tore it open, and stood and read? What would be worse, waking up with Mum screaming blue mur-der, knowing the game was up, or watching while everything fell apart? But maybe it didn't. No, I'm sure it did.

What I've done. Disaster all around. Like, people's lives ruined. Pug's face wincing: 'Your poor mum.' My poor mum. My poor, pathetic father. Poor, pathetic Ricky. Why the hell did they do that? Did they care about us others so little? That's what's sick-ening, their ignoring us and going off together, leaving five indi-viduals without a parent or partner, but without even knowing we'd lost them, still assuming they were there for us. We're like cartoon characters strolling off a cliff into mid-air. How long were we suspended there (*years?*) before I walked in on Dad and Ricky and started falling? Now one by one we'll all realise, and drop—and who knows what'll happen when five people hit bottom? Oh God. *Everything* will change. *Already* everything is different. Between yesterday and today, so much knowing: the blue line across the tester window, the shush of an envelope under a door. Disaster upon disaster, happening so quietly.

Disaster inside me. Leading Pug on to it, really; lying, or moving into a lie; being on the Pill and then forgetting, and not saying, and finally forgetting so often that I'd stopped being on it, and not saying.

I sit up and push back the blanket, listening to the headache, which diffuses forward through my brain, but isn't very strong. My shoes and socks are right there next to the bed; bending to put them on I ignore the apple inside me, ignore it for a bit longer.

Then the gate clashes and I jump up. *It's just a Jehovah's Witness, someone selling vacuum cleaners.* The front door slams. I pick up my jumper and bag.

Pug fills the doorway, in his old black tracksuit with the hood. I'm standing in the middle of the room, red-handed.

'What's up?'

'I have to go.' I head for the thread of space between him and the doorpost.

'You feeling okay?' He closes off the space.

'Yeah, I'm fine.' Although nausea throbs in my throat.

'You goin' home?'

'Yeah.' It sounds like a lie.

'I'll come with you.'

'No! I mean, I'll be fine. I've got some thinking to do. You'd be—I've got to work out what to say to Mum, and everything.' Babble, babble.

He must know exactly what I'm up to. He grabs me with a thump. 'Mel?'

'What?' That little space has opened up again, but my arms are pinned to my body.

'You tell *me* what. When are you comin' back?'

'I don't know. I have to see what happens at home.'

He tries to see my face. 'You were gunna just go, weren't you? Without sayin'. Without leavin' a note. Were you gunna come back?' He shakes me. 'Like, *ever*?' He takes this outlandish thought out of my head and flaps it in front of my eyes.

I look up in shock. 'What?' I try for a scowl of disbelief that doesn't quite come off.

'The way you're acting. Like, you're running away. What's up? I don't mean with your dad and that. I mean with you and me.'

'Nothing's wrong with you and me.' I say it as firmly as possible and look straight into his eyes. *Except that I can't fool myself any longer. I am absolutely on my own. Absolutely, and so are you.*

'Why are you runnin', then? Why are you lookin' like that?'

Because I'm bad for you. Because you were right; I will move on.

His letting go sets me back a pace; there's a thrust in it, of anger.

'Will you let me past, please?' I say quietly, presenting the top of my head to him.

'Will you come back?'

Too long a pause. 'Sure.' I still don't look up.

'Mel?' His voice shrinking. *Beware quietness, where disaster happens.*

I push him aside like a gauze curtain, this man who can stop a 76-kilo fighter. I don't look back. I swing round the post on the landing and thud down the stairs. I'm a coward; I'm running; I'm gone.

I ring Mum from King Street. It sounds as if a corpse answers the phone. 'Yes.' Not even 'Hullo?'

'It's me.'

'Oh. I suppose it's too much to expect you went to school today?'

'I went to a friend's. I had a bad migraine.'

'Right. So you're checking how badly you're in trouble now, hey?'

I laugh, embarrassed. 'I guess.'

She doesn't sound amused. 'Well, I've run out of anger for today. You might as well come home.'

'Is Dad there?'

She snorts. 'You think he'd *stay*? By *choice*? With boring old *me*?'

Pause. 'You *haven't* run out of anger, then.'

She sighs. 'Honey, I'm all over the bloody place. All I ask is, we make an appointment to talk about *your* problem tomorrow morning. I just couldn't face it tonight. I mean face it *again*, because of course we've faced it before, haven't we?'

She just thinks it's the same as last time, where we pop off to the clinic and get me scraped out. She doesn't know about the forgetting, the not-saying, the waiting for and not getting periods. For months. It has to be too late for that 'option'. Which means . . .

'I'll be back in a little while.' I hang up and step out into the night.

When I get back she really looks at me.

'I should've guessed,' she says. 'Here was I going to get you blood-tested for anaemia! And your weird eating habits, of course.'

'Tomorrow morning Mum,' I say. *I* can't face it, either.

She gives me such a hug—more than that, a holding on to.

'I have to tell you that your dad left this morning,' she says, standing back.

'Left? As in . . .?'

'As in went. As in doesn't look like coming back. Left home.'

She's looking into my face, her hands on my shoulders. *I did that. I split up our family.*

I never noticed this before, but the left side of her face has got a very slight sag to it. Her left eye is just the tiniest bit down-tilted, the way our balcony floorboards tilt to let the rain run off the edge.

'Where did he go?'

'To Ricky's place. She called me at work, to explain things.'

'*Explain?* Explain what?'

'I don't know. I didn't listen. I was trying to *work*, didn't want to *think*. Trouble is—' She pushes off from my shoulders and goes over to the dining table, which is covered in files and papers. 'This is the sort of thing I'd normally ring up *Ricky* about, and work it out with her. Ricky being who I thought she *was*, not who I know she *is*, now. I can hardly believe it's the same person.' She stands there with a file in her hand, fallen silent. Then she looks at me. 'I'm tired. And you look pretty shattered too. We'd better switch off our brains and try to get some sleep.'

She follows me up the stairs, both of us moving really slowly. She laughs at our creeping. 'The walking wounded.' It's a joke and it isn't a joke.

2

CONFESSIONAL

*I don't know how they trained. There ain't but one
way to train. Running is the same, punching the
bag is the same, jumping rope's the same, resting,
and going to camp, following the dietary laws.
Clean living is the same. They must have felt like
I felt. It's grueling, it's rough, it's agony,
the training.*

Muhammad Ali

'Not Brenner.' Mum brings her mug of full-strength heart-starter coffee to the table.

'A boy I met last year, before Christmas.' A *boy*. A tiny boy no bigger than my thumb.

'Briefly?' I shake my head. 'That's where you were yesterday?' I nod. 'How far along are you?'

'I don't know. Maybe four months.' Her eyes widen. 'Three. I don't know. I only did the test yesterday.'

Long silence. 'I don't understand,' she says. 'Why only yesterday, if you've been months without a period?'

'I didn't get any other signs, like throwing up or feeling faint. I just felt as if a period was always about to start, and seeing's they've never been all that regular I just . . . I was just expecting one to come, that's all.'

'For three or four *months*?'

'Well . . . they've been a busy three months.'

'I can imagine—keeping up the HSC *and* this secret boyfriend, *and* all that socialising.'

'I wasn't socialising,' I mutter. 'I was seeing Dino.'

'And what does "Dino" think about this?'

I shake my head. 'I haven't told him. I don't want to.'

'You don't want to tell him.' She lifts the coffee and takes a slow sip. 'Any reason?'

'No, no reason.'

'He doesn't beat you up or anything, does he?'

'Oh, no. He thinks I'm the best thing since sliced bread.'

'Why keep him in the dark, then?'

'*Because*, okay?'

'No! *Not* okay!' She stops herself, goes on slightly less fiercely, 'Not okay, Mel, and not *because*. The boy has some rights, you know. You have to have a reason, and a good rock-solid one, for keeping him out of this if you go ahead with it. The two of you made this happen, you know, so don't go taking the full burden on yourself, just to be holy or for God knows what other reason.'

'Look, I'm the one who kept forgetting the Pill, right? And forgetting to tell him.'

'So?'

'Well, it's my fault, then, isn't it?'

'So?'

'Well, you just *said*, about the burden of it—he didn't know he was even *likely* to get me pregnant.'

'So?'

'Stop *saying* that, Mum!'

'Look, accidents happen all the time—pills fail, condoms split, diaphragms get holes in them. The fact is, you get a baby from a mother *and* a father and the father *usually*, unless he's a complete ratbag, takes some kind of responsibility. Helps, you know?' She rolls her eyes. 'Supports. Money, if nothing else.'

'Well, I don't want his help and support.'

She touches her forehead. 'Let me just check with you. We're talking single parenthood here, are we? We're talking Melanie Dow having a child and bringing it up on her own.'

'Well, there are other people. You, and people I'd meet—'

'Me?' she interrupts. 'You think, when I'm just beginning to look life-after-children in the face, that I want to go back to the *nappy* stage?'

'Oh, shit, sorry for spoiling your *life*, Mother!'

'Oh, sit *down*, Mel! It's not *my* life we're talking about anyway. It's this child's. Is there a rock-solid reason why you're denying him or her a father? This is all presuming that you're perfectly happy to be the mother, of course.'

'Well, what's so fantastic about *fathers?*'

Mum watches me curiously, rubs her cheek and settles it into her hand. 'Quite a lot, actually, if you look back over sixteen years or so.'

'Yeah, but for how many of them was he having it off with Ricky?'

'One. One year, if he's to be believed. Since our Easter holiday with the Lewises at the beach house.'

That long! I stare at her, see her eyes fill. She sees me watching, blinks and snatches a tissue from the box at the end of the table. 'Don't get me started. We're talking about a different father here.' She blows her nose efficiently. 'I'd like to meet him.'

'We've sort of broken up.'

'But you were there yesterday.'

'We sort of broke up yesterday.'

She stands up, takes her mug to the sink. 'Well, you'd better sort of get back together again, I reckon. Sounds like you broke up under false pretences. Or did you not give him any reasons either?' She grimaces over her shoulder. 'Did you just tell him *because*, too?'

I sit in mutinous silence. She is too smart, my mother, far too sharp and clear-headed. She doesn't know what it's like to be woolly and confused, to have feelings about things rather than incisive, rational thoughts, to only know things for sure when you look back on them. I'm not going to give in to her pressure; she can be as impatient as she likes. I'm going to wait until things come clear for me, and until then I'll follow my own instincts.

'And another thing,' I say. 'I'm not going back to school.'

My mother is slightly taller than me, but thinner, frailer-looking. Sometimes I can't believe the power she has in her slender bones, her long delicate hands. Her quiet voice: 'You didn't have to get pregnant, you know, to get out of going to school. You only had to ask, and we would have worked out something.'

I get the feeling she's slipped in time, that the 'we' includes Dad, indicates the good old days, the days before yesterday.

'I didn't, I didn't,' I protest. But she makes me wonder.

Boxing is unique amongst sporting activities in that victory is obtained by inflicting upon the opponent such a measure of physical injury that he is unable to continue, or which at least can be seen to be significantly greater than is received in return. For this reason alone many people will advocate that boxing be banned altogether as vicious and uncivilised. Others find some advantages in learning 'the noble art of self-defence' or believe that society is not yet ready to eliminate boxing altogether; they therefore press for rational controls designed to achieve the greatest possible level of protection of the participants.

The weekend is murder. It's like a long dive-bombing mission, this 'discussion'. Mum keeps coming at me, dropping some explosive question like, 'Where do you plan to have this baby?' or 'What will you do for money?', listening while I jitter about, unable to answer, then wandering away, leaving me all in bits, jangling with possibilities.

And there's no normal corner of our lives to hide in now. It's just her and me, a glider and a high-tech bomber, circling each other, with no Dad to ground us. I float along waiting for wind-currents and thermals to point me in the right direction, while she cruises overhead and strikes at random.

Sometimes she loses it. When she comes up against my decision not to tell Pug and sees she can't budge me, she really goes off the deep end. 'You just won't be told, will you! You think you already know everything you need! Well, one day you'll see that you can't just pick up people's lives, turn them upside down and then walk away thinking it's okay because *you* don't feel the damage. One day you'll *feel* it, you'll *see* it, and you'll look back on the way you're behaving now and be *mortally ashamed*!' She had tears in her eyes then, before she slammed out, like a kid having a tantrum.

She can't understand, from the outside. How could she? What's to understand? I don't understand myself. It'd be easy to say, 'Sure, I'll go and see him now.' But when I think of *doing* it, walking that distance, facing that face, speaking those words . . . it just can't be done—not at this moment, not by me.

Sunday night. Rob Lewis, the Wronged Husband, pays us a call. By the slump of his shoulders you can tell how very Wronged he is.

I get to sit in on the conversation. 'It's all right,' Mum says in the special lifeless voice she uses to talk about *the situation*, 'Mel knows what's been going on better than I do. So do your kids, it seems.'

That obviously shakes him—what, hasn't he even *talked* to them?

It turns out that Ricky's booted him out and installed Dad in his place (like a big ugly trophy on the mantelpiece). I'm glad I'm not at school to face Josh and Ambra! Mr Lewis is pretty wrecked. At one point his voice starts going all throaty and he has to pinch the top of his nose before going on. He doesn't actually break down and sob, but if Mum were just a whisker less lifeless and Wronged herself he probably would.

It's awful. They're slumped opposite each other, swapping these awful facts in dull, dull voices. I get them cups of coffee and sit for a while in the combined stink of two wrecked families. *I did this*.

It's a matter of *waiting and seeing*, they decide. We just *sit* for twelve months and as long as we get some respected community member to swear that Dad and Mum split up twelve months ago, the divorce goes through. Rob and Ricky—well, Rob still hopes 'something can be sorted out'.

'What, you want yours back, do you? I don't want mine,' says Mum—it's as if she's talking about a stolen *car*! 'He had his chance and he blew it.'

'This is not the first time, then?'

Mum glances at me. 'No, it's not. The temptation's always been there, in his line of work. Insurance assessors are always cruising around, seeing clients—a bit like prostitutes, really.' God, what an awful thing to say. Awful, but funny—but awful!

As he's leaving, Rob says, 'There's no comfort in being the ones in the right, is there?'

'No, it's just as painful. But it's only a matter of time, Rob. This is the worst of it. It can only improve.'

I think of him walking through the dark to his bare flat, pure miserable pain on legs. How many people do you pass in the street every day without knowing that they are simply anger or sadness bound into a body? It's a lot to assume, that they're all balanced, their emotions reined in to bearable levels. How do you know which ordinary-looking person is the Wronged Husband with the machine-gun, the one to stand in King Street and start spraying carnage around? You don't, you just don't. It could be anyone.

> Primarily the Judge awards points for true scoring blows . . . Boxing is an attacking sport. A boxer strives to win by striking more blows than his opponent, but the blows must be struck fairly, and in accordance with the Rules.
> (a) Scoring blows. Blows struck with the knuckle part of the closed glove of either hand on the front or sides of the head or body above the belt
> (b) Non-scoring blows are—
> Blows struck while committing any of the infringements . . .
> Blows on the arms or on the back
> Soft blows or 'taps' with no force behind them

A working day is a long time. I spend five days learning just how long. Maybe for the first two I keep thrilling to the fact that I'm not at school, that I'll never go back, that I don't ever have to see Lisa again, there in the midst of her group wielding her full strength.

On Wednesday I feel a twinge of panic when Mum leaves for work. The house closes in. It feels like minutes since she arrived home yesterday. I shower and dress and it's only eight-thirty. I read yesterday's paper from cover to cover and it's ten to nine. It's a cloudy day; the light sits at the windows like fog. Oh, God.

I walk to the hospital, a few blocks away. It looks like a prison, or a barracks, but tucked into one corner of it is a doorway marked 'Birth Centre', a picture of a baby curled up in one loop of the B. I go into an empty waiting room. Two women (nurses?) are chatting behind the desk. One looks round immediately.

'Hi. What can I do for you this morning?' She smiles. The other nurse picks up some papers and goes away.

'Hi.' I cross to the desk, not sure what I'm supposed to say. 'I—I'd like to book in to have my baby here.' There, I've said it, to someone official.

She's really nice. She can tell I don't know the first thing about having babies. She tells me there are classes I can take, books I can read (she gives me a list), ways I can find out how many months pregnant I am (something called an ultrasound), pre-natal visits I have to make here. She shows me around the centre. One of the two rooms is occupied, which I find stunning, amazing, with everything going on so normally outside. From behind the door comes a long, low moan, and I look at the midwife in alarm. 'It's okay,' she smiles. 'She's fine. Early stages yet.' Oh, that's really reassuring.

Then when I'm leaving I have to stand aside to let a vastly pregnant woman in a blue maternity smock in the door. *Don't stare.* I force my eyes to her face, which is smiling, perspiring, red.

'Hullo, Marlene,' she says to the midwife.

'What are you doing here, Annie?'

'I don't know! Induce me, induce me!' The door closes behind me on their laughter.

I walk down the street, away from Newtown where I might run into Pug. It's real. I'm going to be as huge as that woman. I'm going to be in there moaning as that hugeness tries to get out of me. How can it? I'll be too little. I'll have to go up to the labour ward, where they have planks with stirrups instead of those nice hotel-like double beds. I'll be sent to the operating theatre and have it cut out of me. I've seen it on television, surgeons' green hands digging in through the weepy red layers and pulling out a waxy, scrunch-faced . . . God, it's impossible to believe. Me. Inside me.

But that nurse sees babies born all the time, and she wasn't shocked or horrified at what I was letting myself in for. 'She's fine,' she smiled at that moan behind the door. She *smiled*. 'She's fine.' How can a person be *fine* with that happening to them?

The lights change and I cross Parramatta Road, semis puffing and pawing to get going again. 'How far gone are you?' she asked me, as if pregnant people fade away to nothing the further along they get, or go deaf and have to be shouted at, or slip into unconsciousness, or turn into giant, mindless cocoons for their babies. I'd believe it, after that woman in the blue dress—I could hardly see her for being aware of her great belly. I'll have to wear those clothes, tent dresses, *drapes*—I'll look like a walking lampshade, all my tassels swinging.

I find myself on a corner looking up at another barracks. The children's hospital. Corridors and corridors, wards and wards, bed after bed of burned, broken, bandaged children, children recovering, children dying, children hanging right on the edge, their parents holding their hands, holding their breath, talking them away from death. Wondrous and unthinkable things going on all day, all night, in there, just like back there at the maternity hospital, and none of it to be seen out here, just a big ugly building almost as bad as the Housing Commission towers opposite. This time next year *I* could be in here, with *my* baby, watching it battle for breath, pacing the lino while the surgeons fix its congenital heart defect.

A truck passes, whirling grit into my eyes. I was right first time around; it *is* too big and scary. The *world* is too big and scary—if we lived in a little house in the country, with no cars around or planes or fires or hard surfaces to fall on or lakes to drown in or murder-suicides or rapists or wars, maybe then . . . If we lived in a Polly Pocket of a world, pastel coloured, round cornered, populated with tiny harmless people . . .

I lean against the traffic-signal pole, my hand over my eyes. I have a very clear memory of myself a couple of years ago standing in the loungeroom in a rage, yelling 'Why did you *have* me, then, if you were never going to let me *do* anything?!' Some day some green-eyed wavy-haired child's going to be screaming at me, 'Why did you have me?' Umm, because I forgot *not* to? Because you didn't disappear of your own accord like your half-brother or -sister? Because it didn't occur to me that you could be real, that you could one month *not be*, and the next *be*? Because I was that stupid (sjupid)? God, if I'm 'too smart for' Pug, what does that make *him*?

The memory of the public is short and the names which have made boxing news are quickly forgotten, to be replaced by those of other simple, ignorant young men with sound brains.

'Oh.' Bloody hell. Dad on our doorstep like a visitor. Looking hunted, fists pushed into his jacket pockets.

'Is Mum in?' He doesn't just walk in past me.

'She's upstairs. I'll get her.'

'I'm here. What is it, Dave?' Mum looks down from the top of the stairs.

'Just come to pick up a couple of things. Is that okay?'

'Depends what they are,' Mum says flatly.

'Just clothes and things. Nothing you'd be able to use.'

He goes up the stairs. I hear him in the bedroom and the bathroom. He comes down, goes to the kitchen, comes out with the things in a plastic shopping bag.

He stops uncertainly by the couch where I'm staring at the TV. I look up and turn the sound off.

'Mum tells me you're having a baby.'

'That's right,' I say, expecting to hear it all again. *Slut. You'd do it with anybody.*

'Whenabouts?'

'November.'

'Phew.' He regards me. 'Hardest thing in the world, being a parent.'

I raise my eyebrows. What does he mean, that I've failed him? That I'm making a big mistake?

'It's the whole point, though.' He starts moving towards the door.

'Yeah?' I turn around in my seat. He'd say *that* and then just walk out?

'You'll see,' he says with a little smile. The door closes quietly behind him, the gate clicks shut. The people on TV mouth at each other.

The ultrasound is like dolphins echolocating in the ocean. You lie down, the operator spreads a cold green jelly on your abdomen, then she beams in sound with a little black handpiece and a picture comes up on the screen. She doesn't warn you, because *she's* seen it a million times before.

Your baby appears on the screen.

There it is.

Perfectly recognisable as a small human being.

'Oh my God. That's me? That's it?' It must be a test pattern or something.

'Sure is. Looks good. See, little heart? The black thing—good strong heartbeat, nice and clear. Oops, lively little beggar. Here we are, top of the head. Thirteen, fourteen weeks maybe. Hold still while I get an image of that . . . Right. Spine.'

'Oh, shit, look at it!' A fragile white S of miniature bones.

'Arms. Legs. There you are, hullo Mum.' The white arm-bones twitch. A twinkle of white fingerbones. 'All in order. Too early to tell what sex.' The handpiece slips across the jelly, the image rolls and a skull-face peers out. Around the curled skeleton the ghost of flesh, within it the black heart blinking white, fast, like a cursor.

'My God. I can't believe it.' I can't tear my eyes from the screen. I can't stop exclaiming. I can hardly breathe.

'It's a baby, all right.' She gives me a brief smile.

Afterwards the receptionist hands me a set of images and a report to take to the birth centre. I rip open the envelope as soon as I'm out the door, but the pictures aren't anything like as good as on the screen. There is one of the skull, and one in which I can just make out the shape of the body, with the head to one side.

> The uterus contains a single foetus lying transversely with bi-parietal diameter 28 mm indicating 14 weeks gestation. Foetal contour appears normal. The placenta is implanted on the posterior wall of the body of the uterus. Foetal heart movements are evident. The cervix appears closed. Thank you for referring Ms Dow.

'The uterus contains a single foetus . . .' It almost sounds disappointed that there aren't three or four! It's all so cool and off-hand; it should say, 'Far out! We looked inside this person and look! We found *another* person, a *fourteen-week-old person*—check out this skull, will you? And look at that heart, that spine, that great placenta, smack in the middle of the wall like it should be! And that cervix, all sealed up and intact. Isn't it a miracle? Isn't it unbelievable?'

I get home somehow. I float through the rest of the afternoon, my uterus containing a single foetus. I go from room to room with this miracle inside me, this moving miracle with its own pulse. When I think about that twinkling hand, and the way the body squirmed in irritation when the sensor pushed the womb wall against it . . . I don't know, I've never had the feeling before. My throat aches, and I'm terrified, and I'm more excited than I've ever been about anything. Not a silly, jumping-up-and-down kind of excitement—a giant, world-sized excitement, immobilising, awesome.

It's just so hard to *believe*! How can we *all* have come into the world like this and just be so cool we never talk about it? Why aren't we all *awestruck, all the time*, at this unbelievable thing that happens when we start? How can everyone just carry on like normal? How come I never knew about it before this? I mean, everybody *knows*, but why doesn't anyone *acknowledge*? Why does all this birth stuff happen in books, behind doors, behind screens of medico-speak? Shouldn't we all stand around amazed, applauding?

When Mum gets home I show her the pictures, try to explain what it was like, because they didn't have ultrasounds when she was pregnant with me. She sits there in her work clothes, looking from me to the little skull face and back. I'm so high on it all I make her smile.

When I finally shut up she sighs, looks down at the image again. 'My grandchild,' she says, trying the word out. She stares at its ghostly face, then shakes her head, and hands the pictures to me. 'I don't know. Anything can happen. Anything *has* happened—I never thought we'd find ourselves *here*, in this situation. You can't help being frightened for the little . . . for little ones like that.' *She knows*. Why am I so surprised? 'But you're right. We are amazing. So complicated. All this from two tiny cells.' She moves her hand in front of me like a metal detector.

'Why didn't you and Dad have more kids?' Today I feel as if it's all I want to do in life, be pregnant.

'I'm not sure. I think we got into the habit of just having one. Everyone we knew who had more seemed to be so tied down and so cranky all the time. It felt right, both of us being only children ourselves. That's what a family *was*—Dad, Mum, child. It seemed like overindulgence to have more.'

The Magninis invade my mind—their noise, their arguments, the crowd of them around the table. I pick up the photo, feel Pug's arms slide around my waist—

'And overwork. Babies can be just hard, physical work.' She

bends to pick up her shoes and her bag. 'Ha! Beside babies, the HSC's a doddle!'

[The brain is] like a mushroom swaying in a small sac of fluid. The point at which 'consciousness' lies is the point where the brain stem joins the main body of the brain, just like where the stalk joins the mushroom.

When the human head is hit hard, the brain sways back and forth rapidly and much strain is put on that precise point. That point acts as a hinge, and each time it sways violently, more tiny veins are torn and many brain cells killed. At a certain point of trauma, the brain will just 'black-out' and the person is knocked out.

There is never a total recovery of these brain cells when the boxer comes to. It is permanent. Mike Tyson will seem to be 100 per cent normal to those around him in a few weeks but in fact, he will only be 99.9 per cent. His reaction time will never be quite as good as it was and his 'hold' on consciousness never quite so tenacious.

It will be fractionally easier to knock him out next time and then he might be down to 99.8 per cent. It will be even easier the time after that. And so it goes.

Next day Mum gets home late because she's been shopping—for presents—for me! She's got me a bunch of books on pregnancy and birth. 'Before you get right out of the habit of studying,' she says, 'you may as well take some notes from these.'

One's about eating and exercise in pregnancy, one's the birth book the birth centre recommended, one's a book of interviews with Australian mothers about their pregnancies and births. I stand there feeling the weight of the books, their shiny covers. I'm overwhelmed. This is Mum's response to the ultrasound— *Okay, time to face reality*. Mine was so different, so impractical: *Wow, this is so amazing!*

'And I bought myself one, too,' she says, pulling out another paper bag and tearing it open. Hers is called *Grandparenthood*.

'Oh, cool, so you'll be able to find out where to get a mauve rinse for your hair, right?'

'Yes, and a pair of spectacles that sit on the end of my nose,' she laughs. 'It might even have some good knitting patterns in it!'

After tea I sit down with the books. Oh God, there is so much to know! It's all pretty scary. The actual birth pictures are—well, mind-expanding. Mum looks over my shoulder and says, 'Well, that's what we're *made* for—to stretch that wide. That's why we're all concertina'd up inside like we are.'

All the people around the women having the babies look rapt to be there—I mean, none of these people are *models* or anything, just ordinary people. The women are *huge*, and most in the pictures aren't wearing anything, so their great big breasts are sitting on their gigantic tummies like cannon-balls, and the nipples are huge and dark—they hardly look real. I don't know how they could stand being *seen*, let alone *photographed* like that.

It's not just the fact that their bodies are so distorted; their faces show a lot, too. There's no smiling for the camera—except afterwards, when the baby's in their arms. You can see pain, effort, distress, exhaustion, and these are just split-second images, no sound, no indication of the length of time the whole process takes—like, how *long* do you have to suffer?

I'm muttering, 'Oh, God,' looking through the pictures. I look up at Mum, all the joy at the fantastic-ness of having a baby inside me burnt off by fear of having it come out of me. I can't believe—but I have to believe, have no choice!—that this will be me in November, that I'll be this size and shape, that I'll be squatting or kneeling or standing there with a baby's head outside of me and the rest of it inside. It just *cannot happen* that that little kicking ghost-skulled creature is going to come sliding out and be another person. But then, where did I *think* people came from before this—a factory production line? Down from the clouds? Why didn't I ever think of them *coming out of people's bodies*? It's not as if I never saw pregnant women, and then saw them pushing the baby around in a stroller—why didn't I ever properly wonder what went on in between?

'It's all right,' Mum says, smiling at my stunned expression. 'You get a big prize at the end.'

'It's worth it?' I say doubtfully.

'Honey-girl, the birth itself is *nothing*, let me tell you.'

'Gee.' *What have I got myself into?* I don't ask that question out loud, though, for fear she'll tell me the answer.

Dad and Mum negotiating downstairs. It's like opening the freezer door, listening in. Cold, cold air. I wish they'd get angry and say what they're thinking, instead of talking about use of the car, and electrical appliances, crockery, CDs.

Mum's got it all sorted out and itemised. Every time she brings up an item, Dad says, 'Oh no, God, you keep all that,' and she says 'I've sorted out your share—it's in the study. I want this to be absolutely fair.' She wants the study cleared by the end of the month. She had a chuckle with me when she was talking about this meeting—'I want the Lewises' house to be so chockablock with his stuff that Ricky can't *stand* it! I want it to be really *inconvenient*—everything's suited him right down to the ground so far.'

'Except Josh and Ambra?' I said hopefully.

'Josh and Ambra are with Rob, in the flat. Ricky and your dad have got all the privacy they want now. More than they can stand, I hope.'

Friday night. It's exactly two weeks since I last saw Pug. I can think about that time, running away from him, without groaning and actually covering my face with my hands, but I still do it in my head. Then I'm lost, don't know what to think. The wish to see him is exactly balanced out by the instinct not to, the voice that says a sharp 'No!' and halts me in my tracks.

The phone rings. Mum's in the bath. *This'll be Dad.* 'Hullo?'

'Mel?' *No, I'm not ready.* 'It's Dino.'

'I know. Hi.' The effect on my heart! I've read you get extra blood when you're pregnant. Your heart enlarges to take on the extra load. Well, it certainly feels bigger, sounds louder.

'Hi. I got your number out the book. Is that okay? Is this, like, an okay time to ring you up?' I can hear traffic in the background. I can picture exactly where he is.

'Yeah, well . . .'

He clears his throat. 'Haven't seen you for a while, that's all.'

'Well, I'm kind of . . . kind of grounded.'

Silence. 'They found out, hey?'

'Yeah, for jigging school and all that.'

'How long for?'

'My dad says indefinitely, so . . . I don't know what that means.' I'm not sure I know what *anything* means, the way my brain's scrambling.

'D'you . . . d'you want me to come round and talk to 'em?'

Oh *God*, no! 'Um, I don't think that'd make much difference.'

'They're really pissed off, huh?'

'Yeah, pretty badly.'

'Shit, I *knew* it was a bad idea, keepin' it all secret like that. You shoulda introduced me to 'em right at the start.'

'Maybe. I don't know.' I really want to *not be having this conversation*. If he'd just come out and ask for the truth, I'd be able to tell him, but as long as he goes on believing my lies, I'm caught in them. And I don't like the feeling.

'Hey, this is terrible. I miss you, mate. I shouldn't've let you go off like you did, all upset, and sick and that. I should've walked you home—I feel bad about that.'

'I feel bad too, Dino. But I don't know what I can do.' That's true enough. 'They're not letting me out of their sight.'

'Bugger it. *Bloody* telephones. I feel like, if I could just get to *see* you, you know?'

'I'm stuck, though. I can't see a way to get around it.' That's true, too.

'There's got to be *some* time when they ease up a bit on you.'

'When they trust me again, you mean?'

'Yeah. As soon as you get a break, Mel, come around, will you?

104

'Cause, mate, I'm . . . I'm goin' a bit crazy here, you know? You know?'

'Feel a bit that way myself,' I admit.

'Yeah? Oh, man . . . this sucks, so much.' I can hear him shifting in the phone box, thumping something with his fist. 'As soon as you can, okay?'

'As soon as I can.'

'Promise me. Shit.'

'I promise. I will. I'd better go.'

I stand at the bottom of the stairs, my hands on the big wooden sphere on top of the newel post, my head on my knuckles, the bones digging in. It's because I'm three months *gone*, I tell myself. The first thing to go must be your ability to make decisions . . . And he would be walking home in the cold, or maybe along King Street unable to stand going back to that room, *going a bit crazy* . . . I torture myself playing back his voice, his breath, evidence that he breathes still, that he hasn't just conveniently disappeared off the face of the earth.

'Who was that?' I straighten up. Mum's all towelling bathrobe and turban at the top of the stairs.

'Nobody.' I know she knows I'm lying.

'Your "young man".'

I nod, sigh, turn away from the stairs, away from her enquiring eyes.

'Any progress?'

I squawk 'No' into my hands.

'What was that?' her voice prods.

'No progress, no progress. Nothing you need to be told.'

'Oh, I'm not worried about *me*.' She goes into her bedroom.

'Neither am I,' I mutter at the ceiling. If anyone ever asks me, I'll tell them my mother coped with the family breakup disgustingly well.

There may be a gradual development of dementia with impairment of memory, emotional lability, slurring of speech and ataxia.

Fatuous cheerfulness may occur, with little insight into the severity of the mental disability, but there may be significant mood swings with irritability and violent behaviour. Tremor, ataxia and spasticity, either pyramidal or extra-pyramidal in type, a condition similar to Parkinson's Disease (especially of the post-encephalitic type) sometimes occurs. The tendon reflexes may be exaggerated and the plantar reflexes extensor. Epilepsy has been described, but somewhat surprisingly, is quite uncommon.

All weekend I'm walking on glass expecting the phone to ring again.

'Come up to Newtown,' says Mum on Sunday. 'I'll buy you lunch.'

I make doubtful noises.

'Come on,' she says. 'You need to get out of this house, out of your own brain.'

'I suppose. Is there anywhere besides King Street, though? I get sick of going up there.'

'Well, *I'll* be there today to make it different for you. How about that?'

'Oh, big treat.' I feel so depressed and fatalistic I hardly even *care* that we might meet Pug.

We don't, and that depresses me even more. I try to eat a mound of salad and drink a milkshake ('a big calcium pill for my grandchild's bones,' grins Mum) while I stare out the window, my eyes flicking from face to face.

'Dave and I made a few decisions on Thursday night that you should know about,' says Mum when her coffee comes.

'Yeah? Like I go to Ricky's place every second weekend?'

She cracks up. 'I hardly think! No, about the house.'

'What, you can't just draw a chalk line down the middle?'

'Very big on the black humour today, darling.' She pats my hand. 'In fact, it could hardly be neater. The house just paid off, the child just flying the nest—'

'I haven't flown *yet*!'

'Officially you have, not being at school any more.'

'Have I?'

'For most purposes. You can stop being a dependent child just as soon as you apply for the single mother's benefit at Social Security. Assuming that's what you're going to do. This is why I'm telling you this, so you *can* decide.'

'What did *you and Dad* decide, though?' I'm not looking out on the street any more. He could park himself with his nose against the window and I wouldn't see him.

'We're selling the house, and splitting the proceeds.'

'When?'

'ASAP, as they say. Open for inspection next weekend.'

I push the half-finished milkshake away from me. 'What . . . what are you planning to do with your proceeds? Fly off overseas?'

'Buy a house. One *I* like. I have to find it first.'

'You don't like our house? You don't want to buy Dad's half?'

'I don't, no, I have to say.'

Long pause.

'What if the house *you* like only has one bedroom?'

Mum smiles, reaches for my hand. 'I don't know, Mel. What if it has?'

'Then there won't . . . then there'll only be room for—for you.' Tears spill down my cheeks. I pull my hand out of Mum's and reach for a paper serviette.

She watches me for a little while. 'This is why, you see, you have to know. Who's going to decide first? Do I factor you in or out of my house? Are you going to strike out on your own or plump for staying with Mum?'

But it's not even *that* I'm crying about. And I'm crying, I'm crying. When she stops talking I put my head down on the table and sob. After a while I feel her hand on my hair, stroking. *Cry as long as you like*, her fingertips say. So I do. I don't try to talk for a long time.

Finally I sit up. She offers me her serviette, mine being a sodden ball.

'It's just . . .' I risk a look at her. She's listening, sympathetic. 'Feel like I've got no-one,' I get out.

'I don't understand this. What happened to all your mates from last year? You *had* friends; did you give them all up for this Dino fellow?'

In a tight, cold voice I tell her what happened to them, where Pug fits in, the way my HSC kamikaze'd. She listens without interrupting once. When I get to the bit about Brenner throwing the stones she turns her head aside for a second, her mouth a thin line. Still she says nothing, until I reach the end, the last time I saw Pug.

'And that was the day I found out about the baby. I went over there thinking I'd tell him everything, but I only got half of it out, about Dad and Ricky, and then this headache got in the way.'

'But you were there all day,' she reminds me gently. 'How long does it take to say "Dino, I'm pregnant"?'

'I couldn't do it, I couldn't do it.' I shake my head and stare at the saltshaker, tears threatening again.

She heaves an enormous sigh, as if she's forgotten to breathe for the last five minutes.

'What was stopping you, do you think? What's stopping you now? Because, frankly, I'm not all that clear why you're not with him now, sharing some of these changes with him. It's not that you've got nobody, so much as you've *cut yourself off*, from some of these people, at least. From Dino, quite deliberately. Lisa— well, as you say, you gave her the ammunition, and Lisa, being Lisa, just went ahead and used it. She wouldn't have the wits to do anything else. Brenner certainly abandoned you; Dad did the dirty on both of us, even though you actually forced the split, when it came down to it—'

'What, would you rather *not* have known?'

'Well, I certainly liked him a lot better when I *didn't* know, and who knows, it might have blown over. He might've got over it.'

'Mum! A *year*, remember, it'd been going on.'

'True. But anyway, that's not the point. You cut *me* off, too, that's what I was getting around to saying.'

'I did?'

'All this stuff you're telling me now, all of this is new to me. Terrible, awful things, things I might have had some power to help you change if you'd only *told* me. Here I was thinking the *HSC* was getting you down, telling myself about the pressure the teachers must be putting on you, when the HSC was just about the last thing on your mind. I really . . . I'm really . . .' She spreads her hands, shrugs.

'Pissed off at me?'

'No. No. Not angry. Well, angry in *some* ways, but not *that* way. I don't—hey, let's get out of this place, shall we? I need a bit of air.'

We walk along King Street in the wind. It occurs to me that if we ran into Pug now I would happily introduce him to my mum. I would be able to do it so that he, she *and* I could all retain our dignity.

Mum takes my hand and pulls it through her arm. 'I'm really wondering where I went wrong, that you didn't feel you could come to *me*, your *mum*—oh, Christ, I sound just like *my* mother trying to finagle intimate details out of *me*! But truly, I feel as if I must've slipped up somewhere, if you couldn't trust me enough to say *anything*.'

We walk up Church Street. I don't feel the need to say anything. I'm just as confused as she is—worse, I'm feeling so woolly from crying, and so relieved at having told her, that I don't really care why I didn't tell her before.

'Was it the abortion?'

'I didn't have an abortion,' I remind her.

'No, I mean the arranging of it. Was I too eager to suggest it or something? Is that why—that has to be—is it?' She stops at the corner of the park and looks at me.

'Is it what?'

'That's why you waited so long, isn't it?' she says softly.

'For what?'

'With this pregnancy. Before telling me. Twelve weeks, they said at the hospital, was about the cutoff point for having an abortion, and it must have been twelve weeks almost to the *day* that your little note came under the door.'

Suddenly I feel guilty as anything, even though I know that— 'I didn't even *think* of that! I didn't *know*, till that day! How could you think that I'd be . . . *plotting* like that . . .?' I'm outraged, panting.

'Maybe you didn't think,' she continues slowly, 'or know what you were doing consciously. Maybe something made you *not* think or know. Some part of you still curious about the baby that miscarried, about the whole process. How does that strike you as a possibility?'

I drop my gaze. 'I don't know, but I didn't work the whole thing out beforehand. As long as you don't think that.'

The park is wide and green, sliced into triangles by paths. It's easy to become small, crossing it among the hooning dogs, the city spread out to the north. The distance makes my eyes strain, used to focusing no farther than across the street. Mum stays quiet beside me, walking, thinking, working things out.

The working week is five times longer than the working day, and there's nothing you can do about it. It's just numbingly, boringly, hopelessly long. When your own company is making you uncomfortable, it's unbearable.

Get out of the house. I do what I have to do. I have my first prenatal visit up at the birth centre. I go to Social Security and apply for the benefit; I cease being a dependent child. When I run out of official business I go into town and window shop, but the arrays of bright goods are beside the point, somehow. I walk beside the water watching the ferries and the tourists. All day I speak to no-one. Even at the railway station the tickets come from a machine. But at least the time passes as the city passes in front of my eyes.

I spend the next few days walking out from home, trying to get beyond the area I know, into other people's streets, shopping centres, lives. Best is being freed from the cramped streetlets of Camperdown and Newtown into the big-blocked silences of Haberfield and beyond, lulled by all the walking into forgetfulness of where I am and how I might get home, wandering through some light-industrial warren of streets with hardly so much as a footpath to walk on, through strange metallic and paint smells, clashes of machinery, past men in overalls loading boxes into delivery trucks, worn signs and skiploads of mysterious rubbish hulking in carparks.

I begin to spend all day out. My mission is just to go, to keep moving, to stupefy myself with all those steps. That's my work. I come home when it starts to get dark, when Mum's there to fill the house. Then we talk and eat together. Then I sleep, long and deeply, without dreams.

Message from inside. I'm lying awake in the moonlight, and I put my hand on where it should be, and it is. Like underground tapping from a cave miles and miles away. It seems so lonely somehow, that it's in there, not knowing anything much, just being. My first memories are from when I was about three—that's so much time to get through before it starts interacting like a normal person. What is it before then? Kind of like a moving, crying, excreting *doll*?

But you can't think like that about that little moving ghost, that movement so small I had to concentrate and be so still myself and listen to it *under* my own heartbeats and digesting dinner. Well, of course you *can*—people kill babies when they're inside them and quite large, and when they've been born, and sometimes when they're half grown up, with cruelty or murder. But I'm just *mad* curious, busting to know, busting to see. In one way. And then, if I look into its face, and see Pug there . . . what then? My brain ices over, my thoughts gridlock. I can't handle it.

The day of the inspection we buy the Saturday papers and go to Leichhardt to wait it out. Mum is calm enough, but it gives me the creeps to think of people tracking through our house, viewing it as an *investment*.

We do our fruit and vegetable shopping and then adjourn to Via Veneto, where Mum settles to the papers and I brood at the window. Part of me really wants to tell her about feeling the baby move last night, but I can't find the right words, the right tone— I don't want to sound coy, or too rapt, or offhand about it, I don't want to blurt it out. In the end she's so focused on the papers that I can't bring myself to say anything.

I'm a stranger to myself, tall, sore-legged, an invisible planet in my middle. I feel as if I'll never smile again.

'G'day, Mel!' It's Luciano coming in with a friend. 'How's things?'

'Oh . . . fine. Mum, this is Lu, Dino's brother. This is my mother Jan.'

'G'day, Jan.'

'Nice to meet you,' says Mum, perfectly friendly.

'You okay these days?' Lu looks at me, quite seriously for him.

'I'm okay.'

'How's the studying?'

'Oh, you know, moving along.' I'm embarrassed, Mum sitting there knowing I'm lying.

'Good on you. See you round, hey?'

'Yeah. Bye.'

Mum has a smile and a frown on her face at the same time. 'I suppose you know what you're doing?'

I lean my chin on my hand. 'Nope. No idea.'

She gives a rueful laugh, shakes her newspaper into position. 'Nice-looking boy. What's Dino like?'

'Nicer.'

'That came back pretty quickly.'

'Nicer looking, nicer person. About the same IQ, though— well, maybe a point or two more.'

She reaches for the sugar for her second espresso. 'Well, you know my feelings about this. I don't know what you're waiting for.' Her eyes are already moving across the newsprint.

His tolerance to all head blows is reduced. After being struck on the jaw he remains dazed for a longer period than formerly and is more likely to be knocked out ('glass jaw'). After a blow on the head his legs will be a little shaky and feel numb. His timing begins to fail and the fighter is no longer as dangerous on the offensive as he had been. His defence, which had been steadily improving with each encounter, becomes less effective, and the pugilist, who previously had been adroit enough to go through a career unmarked, now begins to develop a flat nose and cauliflower ears. Later, his knees tend to give way after a head blow, and a slight dragging of the feet may be noticed, although often only as the contestant is walking to his corner at the end of a round. The fighter still boasts of feeling fine and capable, but now loses engagements which formerly he could have won with ease.

There are two people interested in buying our house. We spend the rest of the weekend poking around other people's houses and flats that are open for inspection. Mum's full of energy for this, but I drag along behind her. I don't want a new house, I don't want everything picked up, moved, rearranged. I want *something* to stay the same. Please?

I catch two trains and a bus to Bondi beach. It's a grey day; a cold wind blows in gusts off the sea. I walk up the cliff path and I'm glad that the wind's there—it'd be a real problem trying to throw myself off the edge.

There is just the wind fluting across my ears, and the planes barging overhead. Hardly anyone's around except old people and dog-walkers. I pass a girl- and boyfriend jigging school(s) together, feel so *old*—the uniforms, and their nervous look, self-conscious. I feel like patting them on the head and saying 'Make sure you use a condom, dears.' It's the one good moment of the day, knowing I'm free of all that.

The rest is numbness. Monday, and a Siberia of empty days ahead. Our funereal house where everywhere I turn I'm saying goodbye to something. You get to know a house when you grow up in it. You can walk through it in total darkness without bumping into anything. You get the restfulness of belonging somewhere. Instead of that I'm like a person being tossed up in a blanket—all around me people are gripping the edges and laughing and throwing me up, getting right into the game, while I fly and fall above their heads, too scared to tell them to stop.

'Your young man came by.'

Mum's sitting in front of the fire. I close the door behind me, take off my scarf. 'What for?'

'To see how you were. To see if you were okay. To find out why you're suddenly incommunicado.'

I'll bet he didn't say *incommunicado*! But I'm not going to go into all this with Mum, not again. 'So what did you think of him?'

Mum pauses, looks into the fire. 'I thought he seemed like a really nice person.'

'You *did*?'

'Yes. He wasn't what I expected at all.'

'No?' I don't want to hear this, I realise. But I *was* the one who asked, so I guess . . .

She looks at me with a glint of amusement. 'Sometimes you talk about him as if he were . . . well, *mentally challenged*, shall we say.'

'Well, he isn't an . . . an Einstein or anything,' I mumble.

'But who is? Only *Einstein* was Einstein. There are other ways of using your brain. I thought he was very together, for a boy his age. Very mature.'

'Mature?' I really, *really* don't want to stand here and listen. This is starting to throw me. Mum's obviously feeling sharp and clear-headed, while I'm stunned and stupid with wind and sea and train-rattle.

'He was also very upset.'

Suddenly I'm terrified. 'You didn't *tell* him, did you, about the baby?'

Mum smiles up at me, so calm and serene I feel sick. 'Would I do that? Would I do that kind of dirty work for you, Mel?'

'It's not *dirty work*! You think I *want* you to? Well, I don't!'

She just keeps looking, and smiling, the firelight in her new short haircut. I can't imagine Pug in here, confiding in her. I want to ask her where he sat, what he was wearing. Did he cry? What *exactly* did he say? 'You're not making this all up, are you, just to make me feel bad?'

'Give me a break, Mel!' She's laughing, with an edge of bitterness. 'You think I haven't got enough on my mind without dreaming up *ways to make Mel feel bad*? You loon!' Then she stops laughing. '*Do* you feel bad?'

I feel disgusting. He came here. He couldn't stand the silence any longer. He wants to know. He's *very upset*.

He was supposed to *disappear*! He was supposed to *not exist* any more! I know it's unreasonable, but I'm still angry. Angry and scared. After all, what does a boxer do when he's *very upset*? I can't imagine Pug upset—it's everyone else around him who gets upset. He's the one who calms them all down, makes them think straight again, keeps the Magnini family running smoothly instead of going up in smoke.

I shake my head to clear it. 'I don't know *how* I feel!' I say weakly.

'Well, you'd better find out before too long, my sweet,' Mum says as I go to the stairs. 'People are hurting while you make up your mind.'

'Oh thanks, Mum. That's *so-o* helpful.' I stamp up the stairs. From the fireside, nothing.

I'm testing myself, I guess. Walking myself like a dog, like the retired couples at Bondi walk themselves, I find myself heading over to Pug's territory. I'm carefully *not thinking* about Pug, the way I've been teaching myself to. I push those little, strong pictures and scent-memories and skin-memories back into their boxes if they stick their heads out. So I'm doing that until I stand in front of the house, which of course is *exactly the same*, except that the frangipani is bare, the yard full of the dead leaves. I get paralysed there. *He's at training. But training's nearly over; Joe might come home any second; maybe Pug's not even at training but up there reading* The Fist*! He could sit up and look out that window any time!* I'm stuck, looking up and kind of wishing, you know?

In the end I do chicken out and go, gradually walking faster as I start coming back to the real world—*God, what am I doing here*?! When I get back to King Street and the crowd I wilt against a wall, having been so stupid and come so close.

And now the house is stuck in my head, grey and run-down like the house of a dead person. I wouldn't be surprised if he'd moved out, unable to keep on coming back to the place. Even living with the raving Magninis would be preferable to that coffin, even tooling around the streets with brain-free Ed. I begin to understand, I think, some of Pug's life, his urge to keep moving, to shape the days, to find a rhythm for them. It's my urge too now, after all.

Having gone through Newtown once, I've broken my resolve. Of *course* I don't stay away. It's too close and convenient, and that's where I go, on a sunny clear winter morning when you'd never expect the worst.

I'm standing at the lights to cross Erskineville Road when he touches my arm. 'Mel?'

'Oh!' I stare at him in terror, in amazement at the reality of him, the actual, three-dimensional existence of him outside my mind. All this time he's been breathing, growing, watching the world with those wide green eyes, thinking. God, what's he been thinking? Inside I cringe.

His face clouds and clears and clouds over again. *We're strangers. But remember all that—? But you pushed me away. Still, seeing you now* . . . His eyes are really urgently trying to read my face. God knows what's written there, but it's as if my willpower is being *vacuumed* out of me, shloop!, and there's only this puppet-body left behind, thinking, *Of course I only* sort of *broke up with him! How could I face* this *and decide never to see him again*?

'How've you been?' Not that I want to know, but I can't stand gawping for ever.

'Okay.' I know an automatic response when I hear one.

People are gathering around us for the next lights. He pulls me by the elbow out of them, not taking his eyes off me. And I can't take mine off *him*, the winter sunlight on his skin, the little scab and bruise beside his eye.

'You goin' out with someone?' he says.

I shake my head quickly—I can't bear him thinking that. But he *has* been thinking that, for *weeks*!

'You on your way somewhere?'

'Just walking,' I say really faintly—it sounds so frivolous somehow.

'To where?'

'Nowhere. Nowhere important.' I know exactly what's going to happen. I'm weak with relief and wanting him, and confusion and resistance and God knows *what* else.

He takes my hand and hurries me home, not looking at me or speaking to me the whole way. I only glance at him a couple of times, half-running along beside him full of scrabbling hormones and emotions.

He shuts the front door behind us, kisses me against the hall wall. I nearly come right there, with the weight of him against me and him being so intense after so many weeks of starvation, of solitude—it's as if he's pouring fireworks into my brain. He's holding me up by my head at the end; the rest of me is melted mush floating somewhere below.

'Come upstairs.' Feel like I'm flying, my feet reaching down to tip the stairs one by one, just to say hullo again.

The room is the way I left it, except light and bright and exposed to the street without the frangipani leaves, a sunlit square on the unmade bed. He kicks stuff out of the way to shut the door, then unwinds my scarf. He undoes my coat buttons, fast and efficient, and I stand there like a doll while he hurries it off my shoulders and bends over to get my hands out of the sleeves. He's still not looking at me. 'Dino?'

He stands up, unzipping his jacket. The warmth and the smell of him flow out and over me, *so-o-o* familiar, so summery I could cry.

He pulls his black T-shirt off. He's not smiling at all—his eyes are staring blank, like marbles. He grabs the bottom of my jumper. 'Putcha arms up,' he mutters.

After a second I do. It's a bit scary. He's never been like this before; always before he was happy to let me lead things. We used to get the giggles when our shoelaces got knotted or our clothes tangled. This is serious.

He drops my jumper on the floor and lifts my chin to unbutton my shirt. He puts his arms around me, peering over my shoulder to see the bra catch as he unfastens it. Small muscles in his shoulder move, millimetres from my nose. I'm really, *really*, *jumpingly* sensitive all over. When he bends and leans his cheek against one breast, undoing my jeans, I have to stop breathing so I don't flinch. Then he pushes me back against the bed so that my knees buckle and I sit down. He kneels and takes off my shoes and socks, and wrenches the jeans off with my underpants caught inside.

'Dino.' I'm still scared, because I'm naked and cold and I can't tell whether he's being rough because he's angry or just impatient. He pulls my knees apart and kneels between them, and presses his front against mine, moving his hands up and down my back. His face is in my shoulder and neck, and then a few centimetres away, the marble-y look all gone. Around his pale green-streaked irises are circles of darker green, solid like jade.

'You feel great,' he whispers.

I'm embarrassed to look at him any longer. I put a hand on his chest. Then he's stroking my hair off my face. His hands follow his eyes, stroking, down the insides of my arms, my sides, up my neck and all over my face. He lays his thumbs on my eyelids and kisses me, runs his hands up and down my cold legs. Everything he does makes me catch my breath. I force myself to keep my eyes open and not groan.

Finally he pushes me down on the bed, the sun in my eyes, and lays himself on top of me. He drags a blanket over us, kicking off his shoes at the same time, and quickly works his jeans off. 'Open ya eyes,' he whispers, and he's there watching as he slides into me. I feel very, very tight.

Then there's a pause. Every tiny sensation is brand new and fiercely familiar at the same time, shocking me with recognition and surprise. *It's been weeks! How did I last? How did I stand it!*

'I'm scared to move,' he says, laughing a bit.

'Why, will you lose it?'

He nods. I listen to our breathing, watch his beautiful face. He shakes his head, shifts his body minuscule-ly, bites his lip. 'Well, this is fuckin' great, isn't it?' he mutters.

I can't stop grinning. 'Yes, it is,' I sputter. I link my ankles behind him. 'Ah,' he warns, closing his eyes. He bares his teeth, I move again, and he comes, giving me a little soft shaky kiss. Present but not present.

And then *I* do, the shivers going right up to the top of my head and out through my toes as he keeps the kiss going. It's one of the strongest I've ever had.

And he knows it, of course. He's staring into my face when I open my eyes, the sun in his hair, reflections of my sunlit face in his eyes. 'Y'okay?' he says in a half-whisper.

I nod and he starts kissing and kissing me. Somewhere along

the way I start crying, and by the time we begin to ⊕⊙ again my hair is wet and my ears are full of water. It doesn't seem to worry him that I'm crying. He just keeps wiping the tears with his thumbs. It doesn't worry me, either. It's not that I'm sad. It's not that I don't want to be here. I've wanted to be here for so long, and not allowed it, for some weird reason. And now that I am, it's more than the sex; the sex is just the first, blind layer of cells reaching out, contacting and welding together, just the (best) outward sign of the whole bodyful being tweaked forward into him, and the larger tugging, of that cloud of me that inhabits, floats above, is dragged around by my body, into the edges of the cloud-self Pug. It seemed so small a thing to withhold, and now the hugeness of giving it steals my breath, forces out tears.

He lies down beside me and will not let go, will not relax his arms around me.

'We gotta do somethin' about this,' he says.

'About what, out of about a *million* things?'

'We gotta get married or somethin'.' Did he really say that?! 'You're not gettin' outa here till we've got a *place* worked out, and a *date*, and a *time*, and a *promise* you'll be there. I can't hack you leavin' and just disappearin'. You get me?' Real anger jabs through the gentleness. He turns my head to face him, wanting an answer.

'Yeah, I get you,' I say, sniffing.

'I *mean* it. You can't just fuckin' *walk off*, right?'

I feel myself going red.

He gives me a little shake. 'I think you like me. I think you like doing this with me, anyway. And maybe more, I don't know.' He's watching me as if he's trying to read some very small writing on my eyeballs. Then he pulls the blanket up over us and really *snuggles* in to me.

'When people get together, like us, you know?' he says, right next to my ear (I nod, wanting to smile, and knowing I *mustn't*, at his *seriousness*), 'Well, they start off, and then they sorta go along together for a while, and then . . . they get to some place where they *both* know it's gotta end.'

'What are you saying?'

'I'm saying'—he takes a deep breath—'that you *say* it's gotta end, but you're wrong. You don't *really reckon* it's over, and I don't either. Nothin's happened that I can see, that means we have to finish it. Unless you're having me on and you really *are* seeing some other bloke.'

'No, I'm not.' I'm trying to think fast. 'It's like I told you, about my parents going off at me.'

'Well, isn't it all—like, he knows now. So maybe we could go on, only with him knowing, like it shoulda been first off.'

'Oh, my dad doesn't care. He's gone now.' I curl my back against him under the blanket.

The bed shakes, and Pug's head hangs above me. 'Huh?'

'He's gone. He left home. He's living with that woman I told you about.'

Pug tumbles down in front of me and claims some blanket, staring. 'What, did he clear out because of you telling him about us?'

I breathe deeply. The truth feels like an express train about to rush out of a tunnel, horn blasting, lights blazing. I can't meet his eyes. 'I don't know. I was over here when he left. That day I was sick, last time I saw you.'

He lies thinking and watching me. 'So that time I called you on the phone, he'd already gone.'

'Yeah.'

'So what you were sayin', like, they were watchin' you like a—'

'It was all bullshit.'

Pause. 'Right.' Pause. 'So what was really happenin', then? Your mum and dad *did* know about us? *Didn't* know about us?'

'Sort-of knew.' Pause. Pug is obviously getting confused. 'I told them it was finished.'

'But it wasn't.'

'But I wanted it to be.'

A snort of disbelief. 'Why'dja wannit—'

'I don't know!' I nearly shout. I can't stand it any more. 'It was—hormones, or nervous tension, or—Christ, I don't know! Now that I'm *here*, *with* you, I just *do not know*. When I was there, thinking my life over, working out what to do with myself, it just seemed like the right thing—you know, it didn't seem like we—' What a performance! Pug is watching so closely I'm sure he can tell I'm covering up something. 'Seemed like we weren't *compatible*, you know?'

Lo-ong pause. *Go on. Spring me. Say you don't believe me.*

'But now's okay?' he says carefully.

'What d'you mean?'

'How do we seem now, to you? Are we, like, "compatible" now?' He moves his face in close to mine.

'Oh, yes. Now we are.'

Pause. Breathing.

'Reckon you'd better stay here, then. Where you know what's what, eh.'

Finally I look him in the eye. I *don't* know what's what. I don't. The path forks right here and now in front of me—*tell him now* or *keep on lying*. I stare for a long time down both paths, but both lead straight into the identical dark forest. Bugger it.

He kisses my forehead. 'What's goin' on in there?'

'Too much,' I say. 'Too much.'

'Looks like it.' He watches. He waits. A long time. Then he says, 'You look all different,' touching my face.

'Different how? Don't tell me. Fatter.'

'No, not *fat*! It's . . . you don't look like you'll blow away in the wind any more, like you did.'

'That's because there's someone else holding me down.' He doesn't understand. 'There's actually not more of *me*, there's more of someone else.'

He takes his hand away. Utter confusion. 'You said there *wasn't* someone else—'

'Not someone else like *that*, you *dope*. Someone else like—'

I try to catch his hand but he pulls it away, aghast at me. 'Like—'
I get hold of it and push it under the blanket, down to my new
solid, anchoring, slightly curved belly, hold it there until he stops
resisting. 'Someone else like that.'

'Like what?' The baby is swirling against the back of his hand.
Can't he feel it? I'm so glad. So terrified. Glad, terrified, glad . . .

'Like that. Inside me.' I can't make it any clearer.

Time stops. The baby swirls and swirls. Pug turns his hand
over. His eyes never leave my face.

'From . . . us?' A voice *can* tremble, saying two short syllables.

'Yes.'

His other hand is behind my head, gripping my hair hard.
'Mel. You know me; I'll believe anything you fuckin' say. Don't
say yes if it's not yes, okay? Tell me straight.'

'It's yes,' I say, looking straight at him. 'There hasn't been
anyone else. It *can't be* anyone else's but yours.'

I see him decide to believe me, the fear easing off his face.
Pause. He gives a mad chuckle. Pause. 'You're blowin' my mind
here, girl. Dead set?' He stares. 'It must be—to be moving—'

'Beginning of November.'

'Fu-uckin' hell. Beginning of November. Fu-uck.' His voice
drops to a whisper and he listens to the baby under his hand.
'Aw, man! You feel that?'

I nod and grin. 'Somersaults.'

He pulls me to him, his face ageing ten years. 'How long've
you been feeling it?'

'A couple of weeks, maybe.' I try to make it sound like nothing. Fat chance. 'Oh God, don't look at me like that.'

'If I hadn't seen you today, but.'

'But you did!'

'I still wouldn't know!'

'But you do! You *do* know. You *do* know.'

'Would you've gone through the whole thing not sayin'?'

'I don't know!' That's one thing I can say with complete sin-
cerity. 'I really, *really* don't know.'

123

We stare at each other, all shaken up.

'Ah, mate.' He scoops me up, pulls me on top of him, hangs onto me. I drop my head beside his and two tears roll up into my eyebrows. 'With any other girl this'd be a fuckin' *disaster*, you know?'

'You mean to say it's not?' I have to laugh a little.

'It's great. It's *great*. You'll never get rid of me now. A kid's gotta have a father, right?'

'Hmm, I *guess*. I guess it doesn't *hurt* to have a father . . . well, it *can* hurt, but it doesn't necessarily *have* to.'

'I thought you were gone,' he says into my ear. 'I thought you'd never see me again, the way things were goin'. Now I find out I've gotta stick around you for another—what? Sixteen, eighteen years? Shit, eh?' I can hear him grinning.

'A life sentence, pretty well.'

'Yeah,' he says wonderingly.

Harding might also have disposed of Giovannini more quickly, having decked him in the 3rd round with a crushing right hook and punished him remorselessly with hooks and uppercuts from then onwards, losing only the 7th round in addition to the first . . . Giovannini sprang out for the 11th round in search of a knockout. For 50 seconds, the two boxers slugged at each other like a couple of street fighters. Then Harding connected with a telling left hook and Giovannini slowed. Another left and his knees buckled. Still another and, mouthguard protruding, he was destined for the canvas. Harding gave him one more to ensure he wouldn't get lost on the way.

It gets dark early, these nights. King Street is cold, and sweet with petrol fumes. I ring Mum from the phone box by the post office.

'Oh, hullo. Where are you?'

'With Dino. I've been breaking the news.' He's here with me; I'm wearing him like a cloak.

'Oh, yes? How did he take it?'

'Pretty well, pretty well. He's quite happy about it, actually.'

124

'Now who would've suspected that?' she says drily.

'Oh, shut up, Mum. Anyway, I'm just ringing to tell you I'll probably spend the night over here.'

'Yeah, well, I guess you two have got a lot to, um, talk about, hey?' She didn't even miss a beat!

'Yes, we have. Lots.'

'Is the boy there with you? I'd like a word with him if that's okay with you.'

'She wants to talk to *you*!' I hiss at Pug.

'Shit. Hullo? Yeah, hi. Yeah . . . I'm pretty rapt, yeah . . . Well, thanks, I guess . . . yeah . . . geez, you don't have to say that . . . oh, that's nothin'. You should meet *my* folks . . . yeah . . . that's okay . . . that's okay . . . right, yeah. Bye.'

He hangs up. 'What'll we get for tea, then? What d'you feel like eatin'?' He pulls me out of the phone box.

'What was all that about? With Mum?'

'Ah, she just wanted to say sorry for not being able to tell me about . . . about you and the baby, when I went around your place that night.'

'Yeah. She wasn't going to make it easy for me like that, she said.'

'Fair enough. I'm glad you told me in the end. I mean, I'm glad just to *know*, but I'm glad *you* told me.'

I'm not used to seeing Pug at this hour. I'm not used to having the whole night ahead of us. I'm not used to being pregnant *to* someone, linked to them, having them know, walking along beside them in the knowledge, their arm around me. Every now and again my lungs give a little gasp of straight untainted happiness.

The shop-lights spill gold across the pavement. Around us wanders a zoo of people, all colours, styles, countries, sexual persuasions, states of health. Down to the last scabbed staggering derro, down to the last sneering dreadlocked neo-hippy, down to the last grubby white pseudo-waif measuring out her life with cigarettes, I love youse all.

3

BIRTHING SUITE

*I'm looking normal. Everyone thinks I should
be very tall, with big muscles. I'm not.
Everything is inside me.*

Kostya Tszyu

The night is fantastically long. Pug's room is quite different by night. The mess disappears and becomes shadows, draped and piled. The window enlarges and fills with frangipani fingers lit up by the street lamp. I notice the trains more, individual car engines along Erskineville Road. Every night is like this for Pug.

He turns over to find me awake, lies there watching me.

'Still can't believe it,' he says for the umpteenth time.

'Wait till it comes out,' I say. 'Then you'll believe it all right.'

He sits up, gropes at the foot of the bed, pulls a T-shirt on. 'You scared?' He lies down again, puts his hand on my belly.

'Yeah, I'm scared. You ever see that movie *Alien*, where the baby alien comes out of the guy?'

He laughs. 'That's a movie, but. That's an alien. We're talkin' a real baby here.'

'But that idea of being busted open. And maybe its head getting stuck, you know, for *hours and hours*—'

'Nah, they'll get it out some other way if you get in trouble. Don't panic. Kids are born every day.'

'It's all right for *you*. It won't be happening to you.'

'I'll be there, won't I?'

'Will you? You won't be up the pub with Ed?'

He huffs. 'You really think I'd *do* that, go off drinking while my . . . my daughter or my son was being born?'

'I don't know you that well. I don't know what you'd do.'

'Well, not *that*. Jesus!' Stubble glitters along the edge of his jaw.

'So it's a daughter you want? You said daughter first.'

'We-ell.' He rolls onto his back. 'Better that it takes after you, I think.'

'A girl won't necessarily take after me, you know.'

'God, I hope so. Aren't many openings for women boxers.'

'Oh, like there are *heaps* for high-school dropouts?'

Pug laughs. 'It's not like you're going to be a dropout *forever*. No reason why you had to drop out in the first place, except the shit you were copping from other kids.'

'That's a pretty big "except", if you ask me.'

'Yeah, but there's other schools, or you can do, you know, a year at TAFE or whatever. That gets you into their courses. I know blokes who done that.'

'Hmm.'

'What I mean is, when you have the baby, that's not the end of your *career* or anythink. Plenty of women have careers and kids.'

'And nervous breakdowns.'

'And shitheads of husbands that don't give them any help. You've got me. What else have I got to do during the day but push a pram round Newtown while you study?'

'Oh, Pug, are you a saint or are you a saint? You'd go nuts.' I sit up, laughing.

'No more nuts than I go now. I'm serious! What's so funny?'

'You would do that? Would you want to, after the first fifty times?'

'Well, would *you* want to? Man, I don't know. Ask me then, see how I feel. All I'm saying is, it'd be a waste not to do something, for a person so brainy.'

For the God-knows-how-manyeth time the future picks itself up, rearranges itself and settles back down. I'm staring out at the fat tree-fingers while this happens, when Pug gets up, crouches in front of me.

130

'Geez, I missed you,' he says. 'I didn't know what the fuck I'd done, where you were, anything. I thought I was better just waiting, not hassling you, and then I couldn't hack it any more. I couldn't hack not knowing, you know? I thought, "Even if she doesn't want me any more, I have to *hear her say it*." So I come round your place. I knew you'd be pissed off at me, but I reckoned that was better than just sitting round hoping.'

The sheets are a war-zone, crumpled, smashed. My heart is wedged in my throat.

'Your mum was great. She's really smart. She was so much like you, too; it was funny, I kept wanting to point it out to her. "Oh, you do that thing with your eyebrows, just like Mel." She was really kind, but. I mean, I felt like an idiot, you not even being there, but she just said, "Come in, I been wanting to meet you", gave me a cup of tea and stuff. She's real easy to talk to; I just ran off at the mouth. It was shockin'.' He's kneeling in front of me, leaning forward, laughing. 'Man, I was sitting there, in this great house, feelin' like, "Jesus, no wonder she doesn't want me, living here, having someone like this to talk to—"'

'You're making me feel *terrible*, Pug—'

'No, no! This's all—because of today. You know? It all cancels out.' He sits closer, puts his legs around me, leans to one side so the window-light shows him my face. 'That's what I'm saying. She's telling me, "Well, you know, Mel's pretty stubborn, but I'll have a word with her," and I'm like, "What's the point?! I'll just go and lie down on the bloody train tracks," and—'

'Pug!'

'—and I see you on the street and . . . and everything just . . . comes right! But, God, for a while there—' His arms are around me, his voice muffled in my shoulder.

I can't speak. Maybe if I hold onto him hard enough he'll feel how sorry I am.

'It was bad, mate. I never felt that bad before. In my *life*.'

My muscles are wires under his weight. The baby comes to a

131

rolling boil. Out beyond the tree, a few pinprick stars tremble in the smog.

Waking up next to Pug. The morning light lies weak and cold on the shambles. I try to imagine how the room would look, cleaned up and with a little cot in the corner, but the mould defeats me, creeping greeny black up the wall beside the dead fireplace. If we *used* the fireplace, maybe the mould would go. But then, the chimney's probably blocked with birds' nests, and the whole house'd go up in flames. And I don't want to live here, in a house full of slobby *boys*.

I turn over. The sky outside is bright grey. It's the first day of winter, I remember. The first day of winter, and the baby will come mid-spring. It's not long, and it's forever; I lie watching the shrink and stretch of time.

Pug draws a deep breath, opens his eyes. 'Hey.' He puts a hot arm over me and works himself closer. 'Definitely we should live together,' he says. 'This is too good.' He dozes off again, breathing next to my ear.

It is good, I have to admit.

When he gets up for training I dress too. 'I've got to go home and get changed. Have a shower. My hair's disgusting.' In fact, I can't stand the idea of waiting here for him, or going along to training. Everything's too raw and real this morning.

'Can I come and see you, after?' he says. 'Like, can we spend a *day* together? That'd be cool, eh.'

Sitting on the bed, I pull on my socks and boots. 'Yeah. Okay.' The smile I give him seems to take a lot of energy.

'We don't have to,' he says gently. 'I don't want you getting sick of me or anything.' I put out my hand, and he pulls me to my feet. 'Like, if you wanna sleep or something. You still look tired.'

'Up half the night, yakking on.'

'Yeah, was great.' He pushes some coils of hair out of my eyes. 'Should do it every night.'

'You should come over. After training, I mean.'

'Yeah, and you go and put your feet up. You right to get over there?'

'It's the best exercise for a pregnant woman, walking.' I pick up my string bag from the foot of the bed.

'Well, take it easy.'

'Geez, get off my back. I'm fine!' I smile to soften the words. 'I'm only pregnant, not terminally ill!'

But it's strange to be upright. After spending so long in that bed, in that room, with that man, I'm cast adrift, floating, off balance. The bleak light ripples like a wobble-board in the sky, and my eyes keep being drawn to gobs of greenish-white spittle on the footpath, smoking cigarette butts, dog turds. People waiting for the buses, walking to the station, all look primped and stiff and unhappy; their soaps and scents and aftershaves are nauseating against the background of diesel smoke. By the time I get to the park I'm sweating, panting from trying to resist it all. My legs are shaking with hunger.

When I close the front door behind me I realise this isn't what I want either, this intense padded quietness. I turn the TV on as I pass, for the illusion of company, and go upstairs. I feel as if I'm covered in handprints, as if Pug's left grooves in my head, pushing his fingers through my hair. I smell, of sex and mould, of King Street exhaust and unbrushed teeth. My clothes are crawling on me. I can hardly steady my hands enough to turn on the shower taps. I strip off, step into the steam, lather up shampoo, soap and scrub and rinse. Finally I can feel my own body, my own self, surface from the grime.

Jeff Fenech of trainer Johnny Lewis: 'I really do love the bloke . . . Johnny has always been there. The day I met him at the Newtown gym was the greatest day of my life. He means so much more to me than just a trainer. I knew he'd never let me get hurt—in or out of the ring—if he could help it.

'That's why I always have my head resting on his back when

I'm going into the ring for a big fight. It's him and me against the enemy and I always give him a little kiss on the back, just to reassure him.'

At the gym, Justin Silva sits next to me on the bench, plucking at his sweat-soaked T-shirt.

'Dino says you're havin' a baby,' he says to me under all the noise. He's never spoken to me before.

'That's right. In November,' I add, just to marvel at the fact myself.

He nods. 'It's really cool having a kid.'

'Yeah? You've got one?'

'I've got a boy, Paul. He's just turned two. He's ace.' He can't stop himself smiling. 'Muckin' around with your kid, there's nothin' like it.' He glances at me to see if I'm listening. 'Guys like, here, they can't understand. You know, Friday night, get off work, you're supposed to go out, have a few, party. Here I am runnin' home to Paul, and Nina, that's my girlfriend, fightin' over who gets to put him in the bath! It's crazy. I love that kid. He's changed my life.' He laughs at me. 'I don't give a fuck what other blokes think any more—and I used to be worried all the time. Just doesn't bother me.' He sits up and takes a swig of orange juice, stretches out his legs.

It's a speech and a half. I'm actually getting a lump in my throat.

'So what was the labour like?' I hear myself asking. 'Did you see him come out?'

'Oh man, don't start me off! It's the one thing that *always* makes me cry. Yep, I was there. I seen him come out. Best day of my life. Just don't ask me for the details.' He bends down and re-ties both shoelaces.

'What about for Nina?' I say, laughing.

'Well.' He pauses, organising his thoughts. 'It wasn't too bad. She went six hours, which is . . . okay.'

'Half the usual, from what I've read.'

'Yeah. It's hard.' He wrinkles his nose. 'Makes you glad you're a bloke, face it. But after, she said it was fantastic. Especially when it wasn't just pains any more and she could do some pushing, help things along. She said pushing him out was just great.' He smiles into the middle distance, then at me. I make a scared face. 'You'll be right. It's just the *best* thing. I thought it'd be shocking, the whole deal, not just him being born, but being, you know, stuck with one chick, stuck with a kid and that. And it does stop you doing some things, but . . . you know, it changes everything. Things you think you'd miss, you just don't give a fuck about any more, can't see why you used to bother with 'em.'

'You want a go, Justin?' Jimmy calls from the ring where he's finishing up with Pug. 'When you've finished chatting up Melanie, that is.' He winks at me without smiling.

It's the first time he's acknowledged me. I wasn't even sure he knew my name, this god of Pug's, director of his life. Suddenly I'm visible—whoa! I just wish I could crawl off quietly under the bench to enjoy it.

Loosening the glove laces with his teeth, Pug sits beside me.

'You didn't waste any time, spreading the news around,' I mutter at him.

'Only Justin, and Jimmy. You're lucky I didn't take out an ad in the paper.'

'You don't want to spread it around. What if I miscarry and lose it?'

He puts a taped hand on my knee. 'Nah, we'll just make another one. Easy.' He laughs and kisses me under the ear.

'Pu-ug! You're not supposed to *laugh* in here, or *kiss* people!' I hiss at him.

'Why not?'

'It's a holy place, isn't it? Sacred ground? Look, no-one else is smiling.'

'That's 'cause no-one else is *happy*. Now give us me windcheater and let's get goin'.'

Selling a house is more complicated than I thought. The agent's busy playing one potential buyer off against the other, and Mum's on the phone to Dad nearly every night keeping him up to date with 'developments'. She's always very brisk and businesslike during those calls, even though when she's telling me about what's happening she's practically rubbing her hands together with glee. She's really into the whole process, tells me every little detail, not noticing that I really don't want to hear, that I just sit like a lump not asking any questions, waiting for her to get on to another subject.

It takes a week and a half to eliminate one of the buyers, and then Mum and Dad go and sign the contracts at the agent's. 'Our last date,' says Mum as she straightens herself up in front of her bedroom mirror. It's nearly two months since I found Dad with Ricky here, and it seems like no time at all. She meets my eyes in the mirror and I can't read hers. Then Dad arrives, also looking too neat and combed, and they go off together, careful not to touch each other.

Then there are six weeks to wait until 'settlement date', which is the date we've got to be out of here, the date 'I actually get my moolah,' Mum says.

'And Dad gets his,' I remind her. 'What's he going to do? Buy a red Ferrari?'

'Don't know. Haven't asked. There may come a time when I care two hoots, but right now it wouldn't bother me if he flushed the lot down the toilet.'

This conversation takes place at the fruit and vegetable market, Mum checking over every cauliflower.

'You never act really upset about all this separation business, Mum.'

'"Act" upset?' She finally chooses the perfect cauliflower and starts pulling a plastic bag around it.

'You know, floods of tears, screaming. Breaking things.'

'You'd like that, would you?' She raises an eyebrow.

'No, but I sort of . . . I think I keep waiting for it to happen and it doesn't. It's like you had a game plan for if you and Dad split up all along, and now you're just going from step to step. Almost enjoying it.'

She gives me a smile that's not a smile. 'Don't worry, I've been doing my tears-and-screaming routine, just not when you're around. And as for breaking things, enough's already been broken, if you ask me. I'm more interested in trying to build things up.' She crosses the aisle to check through the herbs. 'I've seen a few people split up, and I know the damage it can do. I'm not about to let it ruin my life, or yours.'

'How could it ruin *my* life? It's your relationship.' I know that's not what I want to say, but I want to reassure her somehow.

She puts a thick bunch of rosemary sprigs into a bag. 'Don't be daft. He's your father. We had a family. Now it's—it's not gone, it's just . . . rearranged, fragmented? No, let's not fool ourselves. It *is* gone. What it was is gone. Nobody's quite the same person now.' Her hand comes to rest among the celery stalks.

I stand there with the trolley, not moving, hearing her speak my thoughts, my fear.

'You seem the same,' I say, 'only happier. More lively.'

'Well, those are big differences, I guess.' She smiles at me, then picks up a bunch of celery, weighing and turning it in her hands. 'I mean, not that I was *un*happy before, but I certainly feel better about myself after all this than I did before. I just don't want you to think you can't trust anyone, or any relationship. No, it's any *man*, I'm thinking about. Your dad's your dad; he's just one person.'

'That sounds like a contradiction to me.' I nudge the trolley forward and we move along the aisle. 'Fathers can't ever be *just one person* to their kids, I don't reckon. When they start behaving like *just one person*—like, any old person—like, well, having it off with your mum's best friend, it's . . . it's so insulting, like somehow they've just *forgotten* they're your father. Fathers don't do that kind of thing, if they're doing their job properly.'

Mum smiles sadly. 'Nor do husbands, you'd have thought. But it's not just him.'

'No, it's Ricky, *parading* around our house in skimpy clothes and no bra—'

'I was going to *say* . . .' She waits for me to cool down. 'Maybe I wasn't working all that hard on my relationship with your dad. Maybe with that, and with you getting to the age where of *course* you'd look beyond the family for stimulation, he felt that our family hardly existed anyway.'

'Well, he should have *told* us, then, if he wanted us to lift our game.'

'And we would've said, "Sure, Dad, no worries", without taking offence?'

We look at each other. Our guilty laughter brims and spills over.

'See?' says Mum. 'You look at it one way and he's the devil incarnate. Another, and the poor guy didn't have a chance, living with two stubborn cows like us. Oh, I don't know.' She starts picking over the green capsicums. 'We all got a bit smug, I think. Tried to ignore the big changes. In you, him, all of us. We just sat there while the ol' lemonade went flat, doing nothing. Who wouldn't want out?'

'I still think he should've tried.'

'Maybe he did. Maybe we didn't notice.'

I'm disconcerted. 'You reckon we're that bad?'

'It's not a question of good or bad.' She puts the bag of capsicums in the trolley. 'It's just, I don't know. Life, human nature—those big things nobody understands. Now, go and get in the queue at the deli section. I'll be with you as soon as I've got the cucumbers.'

Another fight night.

I was a bit nervous about seeing Pug's parents after the baby news, but I needn't have worried. They're over the moon about it. His dad gives me strict instructions to have a grandson, and

138

his mum hugs me over and over again, smiles up at me, hardly able to speak for imminent tears. Then Oriana pulls me aside, alight with curiosity, wanting to know what it feels like, bursting out 'Oh, it's so *exciting*!' every minute or so.

'I thought everyone would be angry with us,' I tell Mrs Magnini later when we're out in the auditorium waiting for the match to start.

'Ah, no. I have my first baby Luciano before we get married. Seven months after the wedding, here he is—nice big baby, can't be early! Everybody know! Anyway, today is different: people live together, no marry, have babies, no marry.'

Pug's team comes down the aisle to the ring, Pug in the middle, a splash of hot red in the middle of a motley crowd. His mother puts her hand on my arm.

'I always know Dino have the first grandchild. I always know. Looking at Luciano—' She shakes her head, her bottom lip stuck out. 'At Oriana—' Same shake, same face. 'Then Dino come along and I think "This is the one. This boy the steady one, the family one." Always very good with the children.'

Her son looks out at us over the foaming applause, his face rigid with pre-fight tension. I feel as if, if I just knew the right words, the right *spell*, I could snap us both out of this odd, vicious dream and back into the real world, somewhere where he could move slowly, without calculation, somewhere where he could spend his days being 'very good with the children', away from the glare of all these people, their obsession with this game, their hanging out for blood, anyone's blood.

In the month we weren't together, this was one thing I didn't miss, being made vulnerable by Pug's being vulnerable, this naked, feeble hope that he *won't get hit* this time around.

The crowd chills to silence. The team melts off the ring. Two pugs hover there, super-brightly lit, clean, dry, mouthguarded. I close my eyes and lock my brain until the bell sounds; then I have to watch.

Women have been excited by the spectacle and occasionally have swelled the audiences for certain fighters ... but their participation has always been peripheral, even discouraged ... Few fighters' mothers and wives have been enthusiastic about their menfolk's trade, they prepared too many soups for bruised and battered mouths, changed too many dressings on lacerated faces. The women have always provided newspaper copy for anti-boxing articles.

'It's me.'

'Did he win?'

'Of course he *won*, Mother!'

'Of course! Is he okay?'

'Not a scratch. The other guy lasted one and half rounds. Of eight. It was almost insulting.'

'Wouldn't like to be *his* girlfriend, eh?'

'No.' I laugh, in relief. Relief at Pug's victory, relief at being able to just ring Mum and *say*, tell her *straight*, what's happening. 'So we're heading back to his parents' place for supper. By the way, they want to meet you, now that you're practically related. Sunday lunch, his mum suggested.'

'I'll be in on that. Will I see you before then?'

'Umm . . . I guess it's possible.'

'Coming house-hunting tomorrow, for example?'

I shift uncomfortably. 'Mind if I say no?'

'Ooh, a bit. But if I find anything *wonderful* I'll force you to come round and admire the outside of it later on, okay?'

'Okay, that's fine. It's all the *non*-wonderful places that get me down.'

'Fair enough. Congratulate Dino for me.'

'I will. See you later, Mum.'

The following weekend she does find something wonderful. 'It's just come on the market,' she raves at me when she gets home. 'It's up for auction, but I've made them an offer. It's gorgeous, Mel! I couldn't believe my luck when I saw it!'

And even I have to admit that it's heaps better than any of the other places she's dragged me through. As she says, it's like a country cottage dumped in the inner city, quite a cute weatherboard place, grey, verandas on three sides. It looks as if the owners got halfway through renovating it and ran out of puff—the kitchen and bathroom are quite trendy in a consciously old-fashioned way, but the other rooms still have their old paint, and worn red carpet. 'The beauty of it,' sighs Mum, standing in the middle of the loungeroom and breathing deeply, 'is that there's no smell of damp. And all the work under the floor's just been done, new stumps, new bearers in a few places. I can't go past it. Isn't it nice? And the garden—after that poky little courtyard and the little hanky of lawn, it's like a—my imagination just goes into overdrive, thinking what to do with all that space!'

'It's pretty good,' I say grudgingly as we stroll around the outside. 'A bit far from everything, though.'

'Come on, with Stanmore station just down the road? And we're *two* minutes from Leichhardt instead of a whole *five*!' She's trying to joke me into feeling as good as her.

I feel weird, though, as if I'm the cautious old mother and she's the crazy daughter wanting to move out, grabbing the first opportunity. I feel as if I ought to warn her not to get too excited, that the deal might fall through. Most of all I feel as if she's not treating our old house with the proper respect. It's the only place I've ever lived in and here she is shrugging it off, her mind on the cash and the next place, not looking back at all.

We'll be looking in the photo albums saying, 'Oh, there we are in the old place. There you are with Dad, on the balcony,' and it'll be a whole *era's* distance from where we are then, with this scungy garden tamed and blooming, with our things—and some new ones replacing Dad's share—positioned throughout the rooms, and the baby . . . somewhere. Where does the baby go? We'll have to fix that front fence or it'll crawl out into the road. We'll have to put shade-cloth or chicken-wire around that verandah rail, get gates for the steps. I pause in the front path, feeling heavy and listless, overwhelmed by just *those* preparations. Maybe this isn't the right place, for me and my child. And Pug's room isn't right either. Maybe nowhere is right. Maybe we're just unwelcome in the world, the pair of us.

Everybody knows everything now—Mum and me about Dad and Ricky, Mum about Pug, Pug about the baby. You'd think everything would be fantastic, with all the truth out, but it's not. I'm still floating, being swirled down towards some terrible dark plughole. Is it the baby being born that I'm scared of? That's part of it. I'm starting to show, to round out, to be conscious of how much time there is to go, how much bigger I'll be by November. But that's not the core of it—that's made up of a torn, frightened feeling centred on this business of Mum's new house, on the Magninis and Mum getting to know and like each other, on Pug and that intense look he gets sometimes, full of unsaid things, pleas, difficult truths. People all around me are protecting me from themselves: Dad saying 'Don't come in!'; Mum doing her crying and screaming out of my sight and hearing; Pug holding on to something. It makes me wild with anger but at the same time I don't think I've ever felt more in need of protection—frail and clumsy, completely unable to cope. Like a newborn.

Pug's at home with me, fixing up my old bassinet in the back courtyard. I'm making tea, raspberry-leaf and mint tea, because Mum says raspberry-leaf's 'good for the womb', even though it sounds and tastes like witch's brew. There's a knock on the front door. Dad.

'Oh. Hi.'

'Hi. Hoped you'd be in. I just want to borrow the projector. It's okay, I've teed it up with your mum,' he adds ironically as I hesitate. I step back, and he comes in.

He's lost weight. He's got new clothes. He looks almost . . . almost *trendy*? My father?

'Ah, bugger it!' Pug says loudly out the back.

Dad grins. 'Sorry, have you got visitors?' he says very *delicately*.

'Only Dino,' I say, hoping he'll think it's . . . I don't know, the gardener or somebody.

'Oh yes? Mind if I go out and say hullo?'

'No, go ahead.' I quake in my shoes, following. It's all happening too fast.

Pug's squatting by the bassinet stand pieces, scowling and sucking a pinched finger. 'Dino, this is my father, Dave. Dad, Dino.'

They shake hands. Pug looks so alert and polite I could *eat* him.

'Having a bit of trouble with the Family Heirloom?' says Dad, giving the frame an amiable kick.

'Yeah, I can't work the bloody thing out. I mean, if I could see it set up I might be able to suss where everything goes, but I'm workin' in the dark here.'

Dad walks around the scattered pieces. 'Buggered if I can remember,' he says. 'Ferret us out a photo, would you, Mel? I think *this* is a part of the stand as well, Dino. See, if you don't have the little struts in position . . .'

When I get back they're crouched one on either side of the frame, lifting pieces and looking at them like chimps in a lab. 'Oh God, I remember all these little L-plates. I hope you've got all day for this.'

They pore over the photo. It shows me propped up in the bassinet like a doll, the flash making red discs in my eyes. But they're not looking at me.

I fetch my tea and sit on the flower-bed wall, watching them piece the stand together. The man in my life and the man who walked out of my life. I'm split exactly into three as regards Dad: I hate and am disgusted by him; I feel exactly towards him as I always have; I'm poised feeling nothing for him, waiting for something he does or says to show me my *real* feelings for him.

143

And this is only one person we're talking about! This world is certainly not a simple place.

You would swear Dad and Pug were old mates. They relate on the completely practical level of getting this bassinet set up, as if the thing had no sentimental associations, no links with a life Dad went ahead and destroyed, or with a life that exists inside of me that's going to change everything for all of us all over again. It's just this-goes-here and this-attaches-to-this, wood and metal bits in the right positions, emotion-free, significance-free. While I sit here growing bigger, almost *bubbling over* with significance.

'So that's your Dad,' says Pug when I come back from seeing Dad out. He's crouched in the yard, putting the wheels on the stand.

'Yes.'

'He's all right.' Pug works on, looks up at me. 'I'm not saying what he went and did was all that fantastic, but he seems to be an okay sort of bloke.'

'Yeah, he's okay,' I say lightly, wishing I could look at Dad so straightforwardly, wishing I could care so little, wishing my days weren't so clagged up with feelings crossing each other like riptides.

Ivy covers the back of our house. Ivy covers the fences. Not a leaf moves. It smells green. It blurs edges and fills corners, making everything look soft and ruined. The sky is far and blue, as if seen from the bottom of a ruined tower.

Pug's smiling at me. 'Still pissed off with him, aren't you?'

'I'm not supposed to be?' I swallow a mouthful of cold, bitter tea. My mouth twists.

'Well, your mum seems to be . . . you know, working herself out.'

'Mum's Mum. I'm me.' I glare back at him.

He smiles again. 'Aah, it takes time to get over shit like that. Don't rush yourself, it'll happen.' He stands up and sets the bassinet on its wheels. You'd never guess, now that it's all together,

144

just how many tiny fiddly pieces went into it. Pug stands back from it, and we go all quiet.

'Bloody hell,' he says. 'You used to fit in that.'

'Yeah, and now look at me—the size of a house.'

'I didn't mean *that*.'

'I *know*.'

'It's just—it couldn't be for anything else but a baby, could it? A baby *person*.'

'It couldn't. You're right.'

I'll remember this: us caught here at the bottom of the tower with this thing made of wood. The heavy, ivy-covered silence, the only movement Pug's eyes, green in the green.

We're walking up to Newtown, through the park. They're lounged on a bench by the swings, smoking, two people the sight of whom used to send me down into darkest despair. By their stillness I know they've noticed me. The path goes right behind their bench.

It's when I see the consciously casual way Donna puts the cigarette to her mouth, the way she squints against the smoke, her bitten nails, that it strikes me—the bliss of walking past them, and feeling nothing, no fear, no anything. They could be trees, a seesaw, garbage bins.

Just before we're out of earshot I hear Donna say with deliberate clarity, 'Stupid moll.'

I feel Pug tense up beside me, but he follows my cue and keeps walking. 'D'you know them?' he says, a little way on.

I grin up at him. 'No.' It's as simple as that.

'Go gently with that box, Mel,' says Mum, standing aside.

'It's only books.'

'I mean gently on *you*, duffer, not on it. It's not worth losing a grandchild over.'

'Oh, *that*.'

'Yes, *that*.'

I put it down and go out to the ute for another load.

'Hey, give us that.' Pug comes up the path.

'I'm *okay* with it.'

'*Give* us it. Take something lighter. Take that box of stuff for the kitchen.'

'Bloody hell! You're all carrying on like I'm *incapable*.'

He grins. 'You gotta look after yourself, mate.'

'I *am*! I'm *fine*!'

'Good.' He blocks my way, takes the box from me, leaves me swearing by the ute.

'Hey, we're almost moved,' says Mum when she pulls up with the next load.

'Yeah, all we need is some beds to sleep in.'

'Well, they should arrive any minute.' She hands me a lampshade and the three Balinese fans she used to display on the bedroom mantelpiece. 'I've got Bob Close keeping an eye on the movers while they load up. Where's that tea? I'm ready to drop.'

The three of us sit on the veranda.

'It's really clouding over,' says Mum. 'Hope it doesn't rain on our beds. You should see the old place, Mel. It's starting to echo, it's so empty.'

'Don't *talk* about it!'

'You sentimental old thing.'

'*Shush*, Mum!' She sees I'm serious and shuts up. Pug looks from her to me, surprised. 'Don't ask. It's nothing,' I tell him.

'Whatever you say.'

It's cold outside, for someone who's only been allowed to carry fans and teacups. Now that the sun's gone everything looks incredibly dreary, the 'quiet cul-de-sac' Mum was so pleased to be living in now seeming lifeless, deserted. The only sound is the distant traffic mumbling, and slurps of tea.

'Well, better get back to it.' Pug puts down his mug and goes up the path.

146

A jumbo jet lumbers low overhead. 'Cathay Pacific' reads Mum and sighs. 'Yep, there's a whole world out there.'

We watch the plane cut through the clouds and disappear. 'Maybe I should've taken that overseas trip you suggested.' She watches for my reaction.

'And when you got back?'

'Maybe I wouldn't've come back. I could've made a new life in Kashmir, or Barcelona. *Tuscany.*'

'Well, why *didn't* you?'

She thinks for a while. 'Too much of a coward. For the moment, anyway. Maybe when I'm a bit further along paying off this mortgage ... Hey, there's nothing like watching other people work, is there?' she says as Pug passes us with another carton.

'You're right. You stay there. Have another cuppa.' He disappears into the hall.

Mum squinches up her face at me. 'Is he a doll?'

'He's useful, isn't he?' I joke.

'He's lovely. I don't know how such a curmudgeonly old stick as you managed to get hold of him.'

'I must be nicer than you think.'

'There they go, two men and a baby van.' Mum peers out through the curtain of rain at the edge of the veranda. The noise on the tin roof means she has to shout.

Now the house is dark. It feels as if I'm crawling into a burrow going down the hall. Pug is restacking the book boxes in the loungeroom, which has about a two-watt globe in the ceiling light, so that he looks like a smuggler sorting loot by candlelight. All today I've found myself drifting towards him, needing to know where he is and what he's doing, then hitting a patch of restlessness and having to move away again.

I hate this, these bare beds, this not knowing where anything is, not being able to walk through the house without dodging cartons and stepping over stuff. Now the rain's trapped us in here, the way night-time does only pale grey and noisy, beating on the roof. If everything was sorted out it'd be cosy, but with all the doors open, the cold air coursing through and the crowd of things to be sorted it's like moving through a bomb site.

I go to 'my' room and start clearing the bed of clothes, very few of which fit me any more. I stash them away in the cupboard, hunt up some bed-linen and make my bed. I set up my lamp on the bedside table, and as soon as I switch on its white-gold fan of light the whatever that's rattling around in me, making me want to cry, stops. I fit my bookshelf into the space beside the fireplace and start stacking, all the pregnancy books, all the school books, all the storybooks reaching right back to a few tattered Miffys from earliest days. Some of these I haven't seen the covers of for years. I get absorbed, putting them in alphabetical order, reacquainting myself with them, sitting in my corner with my baby keeping me warm.

'Got it looking nice in here.' Pug comes in and sits on the bed. 'Mind if I move in?'

'Sure, go ahead.' I look up at him. 'Are you serious?' I ask, seriously.

'Nah. Well . . .'

'Well, *yes*, you are.'

'I think about it, that's all.' He examines the palms of his hands, then looks up. 'I wonder what *you* want.'

'Oh, so do I, don't worry.' I push in the last few books, kneel up and walk on my knees to him. 'What do *you* want?' I say.

'I've got it already. More. Bloody hell.' He puts a hand on the baby.

'What do you want for later, though? In terms of where we live, things like that?'

He shrugs. 'Geez, Mel, as long as it's "we", I don't give a rat's where we live.'

'Oh, well, that's a nice way of putting it,' I laugh.

'Honest, I don't care. I don't care if we're in a *cardboard box*!'

'I mean realistically. God, Pug, you're such a romantic! Get your feet down here on the ground.'

He crosses his ankles behind me, puts his hands on my shoulders. 'Mate, if you want me here, I'll stay here till you kick me out. If you want me over in Newtown, that's where I'll be. If you want me to bugger off completely . . . well, dunno about that one—'

'I don't think I want that one.'

'Anyhow . . . pretty well any other thing you want, I can come at it. Just say.'

'Do I have to decide right away?'

He shakes his head. 'No, I'm happy just cruisin' along like this. Everything's gunna change in four months anyway, so . . .'

'Three and a half.'

'Three and a half! Shit a brick, hey?'

'More like a shit-a-watermelon. Oof!'

He holds me tight, doesn't say anything. I close my eyes and rock there against his shoulder.

'It happens every day, mate,' he says into my hair. 'One day it'll happen to you, and the next day it'll be over.'

'And we can start all over again.'

'Yeah, I was thinkin' about that the other day. We started so early, we could probably fit in about twenty kids.'

'Oh, *cool*! What a *fab* idea! God, I'd hate to see my body at the end of it—like an old busted balloon!' I draw back laughing. 'But I'd always be beautiful to you, wouldn't I, my love?'

'You probably would, if I could *find* you with all those kids runnin' round.'

'Oh, God, what a picture! And you'd be completely out of it, after too many fights trying to keep us all fed and clothed!'

'See? Things aren't too bad, are they?'

'What do you mean?'

'Having just one baby starts to look, like—'

'Easy-*peasy*!'

'No problems. We'll be right.' My laughter winds down as I look into his face. 'We will,' he says. 'Honest.'

The weeks aren't so horrifyingly long now, not now that I'd like them to slow down a bit and let me think straight. August arrives, and nothing resolves itself. My mind seems to be shrinking as my belly gets bigger; I can only hold very small thoughts in it. Every time I go out I forget one vital thing, like my list-of-things-to-do-while-I'm-out, or my house key, or my wallet.

I stop caring about anything much. I walk, and sleep, and eat, and grow. I sit and listen to the baby. I'm off away from everyone in a hormonal trance. I'm not a person any more—hardly any of Mel-from-before exists now. She's just a self-contained hydroponic farm, sluicing all the right chemicals through her system, the switching and mixing networks operating on automatic.

We start going to the birth classes up at the hospital, and find out more about how this farm works, how the muscles will contract to push the baby down, how the bones may actually separate to allow its head through. In that class I suddenly feel normal in shape, in fact quite slim—some women are due to have their babies just after the classes finish in six weeks' time. We are the youngest people there, but it's funny, nobody seems to notice. We're all 'gone' in the same way, our old identities fading but nothing new established to fill in the gap. Our heads are full of unseen, internal things, fears that our bodies aren't up to the task, blank disbelief that there are seven invisible extra people in the room with us as we rattle on about herbal teas and sacro-iliac pain and water births, and gigglingly practise birth positions and relaxation exercises.

When we walk home to Pug's place afterwards, often we're silent. 'There's a lot to get your head around,' says Pug, and we'll wander through the dark together, trying to get our heads around it, dazedly watching the Thursday-night fun crowd milling along King Street. I feel calm, content, important in contrast. When we get home we might talk until past midnight, or we might say nothing and go to sleep. My sleep these days is like a long soak in warm black ink; it's hard to shake all the drops off when I've woken; it's hard ever to feel fully awake. At the birth classes I'm at my most alert, because all this information matters so much, but for the rest of the time I'm zombie'd out, almost a danger to myself, liable to step off a kerb without bothering to check the traffic, to leave a kettle on the stove until the hot metal smell reaches me dozing in my front bedroom.

Then September comes. Spring. The air grows soft, and smelly with sweet rotting jasmine, great swags of it over the fences between the hospital and home. I'm getting big out front, but from behind you wouldn't even know I was pregnant. Now I can tell not just when the baby's awake or asleep, but which way it's lying. And what's weirder, Pug can too. 'See? A foot,' I say, and we watch as the little bump moves around and then disappears under my ribs. Or the whole baby will squirm about trying to somersault the way it used to, trying to get comfortable, and we'll stare at it, and hold it, guessing which bits we can feel. 'Doesn't that hurt?' says Pug, amazed.

'Only if I don't sit up straight, or when it butts my bladder with its head.' Otherwise it's nice, scary but pleasant. I can't help feeling proud of it, even though I can hardly take any credit for the system working so well. I walk and walk, sailing around the streets. I come home and nap, wake up when Mum gets home, cook us some dinner, go for an evening stroll with Pug. If life could go on like this, vague, untroubled, unchallenging, not forever, but for longer than two more months . . .

We are sent away for a week, like a pair of parcels. Mum lends us the car and Pug drives us down to the beach house. The house still belongs to Mum and Dad; they've decided they can bear to share it if the alternative is giving it up completely.

So we get a taste of living together, in a sort of fantasy. We swim in the cold, cold sea, walk the thundering surf beach and the smaller bay beach, and the reserve with its soft tough matted grass and its sinuous dark trees branching out at the top like feather dusters. We breathe live air, watch galahs and lorikeets at the bird feeder, go barefoot everywhere, sleep long nights with the baby kicking between us, hardly speak. We eat when we feel like it—new season's fruit, bread bought daily from the hot bread shop, pasta, salads. We have breakfast in bed every morning, and watch the sunset every night from the point.

On the last evening we're down at the surf beach. Pug walks up from the water, the horizon at his ankles, the seawater clinging all over him. I'm sitting like Buddha, straight, relaxed, my lump just touching my thighs.

'Why don't you ask me to marry you?' I say.

The breeze and the sea-thunder must have made him deaf. He picks up his towel, rubs his hair dry, and his face, sniffs his dog-snarl sniff a couple of times. Yes, he mustn't have heard.

He throws the towel on the sand, sits on it. Hugs his knees. Wipes his nose on his wrist. 'Why don't *you* ask *me*?' he says casually, out to sea.

'Is it something you want, us to be married?'

'It wouldn't be like this, you know.'

'Like what?'

'Like here at the beach.'

'You haven't answered my question.'

'I'm not going to.' He gives me a cheerful smile.

'Why not?'

He shrugs. 'Dunno. I'm superstitious.'

I laugh. 'Superstitious about what?'

'About talking about getting married, with you,' he says into the back of his wrist.

'Well, who else are you going to talk about it to?'

He just smiles at me.

'Come *on*.' I put my lips against his bare shoulder, taste the salt. 'Oh, *come* on, Pug . . .' He puts his head down. I peer up at him under his arm; his eyes are closed, his mouth half-smiling. 'Pu-ug! Pu-ug!'

'I'm not gunna. Leave me alone.'

'Pu-ug!' I wrap my arms and legs around him, kiss up and down the back of his neck. '*Please* talk about getting married. *Please!*'

He shakes me off. I fold up like a flicked spider. 'Look,' he says quickly. 'If you and I got married, all you'd wanna do is get free of it. It costs a lot of money—the way *my* family'd want to do it, that is—and it means fuck all, in the end. It doesn't stop one person leaving the other one. Now stop—stop stringing me along. You asked, and that's what I think, okay?'

'Okay, okay! How do you know what I'd want, anyway?'

Already he's embarrassed. He falters. 'I know, okay?' He ducks his head, waves an arm, Italian for *I'm lost for words*. 'I watch you. I listen to what you say. I spend a lot of time with you. I spend a lot of time trying to figure you out. I may not be all that smart, but I do know *some* things.' He scratches the ear closest to me, glances at me staring at him, gets up. 'I'm going back up the house.' He snatches up the towel. 'You coming?'

'I will in a minute.' I sit there like a stone while his feet squeak away in the sand. It's getting cold, the light turning blue. I wrap my wet, sandy towel around my shoulders. My stupid, pregnant brain tries to hook onto a thought, but they fly through too fast. I end up gazing at the waves, the way they zipper themselves closed the full length of the beach, the way the yellow froth bounces and skids up the sand.

Then Pug's hands are on my shoulders, pulling me backwards until I lie on my back. His face is above me, upside-down. He kisses my mouth, then looks at me eye to eye. Water hisses and crunches, and wind glides.

'You're like my mum,' I say. 'You know me too well.'

'I think your mum's fantastic. When I look at your mum, I know you're gunna turn out all right.'

'What, even though I'm hopeless now?'

He nods. 'Even though you're a complete fuckwit now.'

'Oh well, that's good.' I roll my eyes. 'That's something to look forward to.'

'Get up,' he says. 'Come home.'

I start to laugh. 'What, so you can *jump* on me?'

'So we can play a game of *cards*, deadhead.'

He helps me up the beach. I'm laughing so much I forget to think *Goodbye* to the sea.

The last dawn here. Lying together all three of us, the other two asleep. Who'll be next in this big double bed? Dad and Ricky? Mum and . . . some new boyfriend? Us again, with the born baby between us?

Last time I was here I slept next door in the single bed. I was boiling with anger at Dad, missing Pug, going over that first fight in my mind time and time again. Two months pregnant, maybe, and not knowing. Younger. Sillier. Still at school, still frightened of Lisa, still frightened of all those *kids*. Frightened of everything, except the truly most frightening thing of all, the thing inside, growing, getting ready to overturn my whole life, rip it open like a bag of Smarties, spill it in all directions.

Go with your body, says Fiona, the woman who runs the birth classes. *Listen to your body, work with your body.* Sometimes I feel as if there's not much else to listen to, not much else my mind can take on. Every thought I have seems to disappear in a crowd of echoes, connections and questions growing bigger and bigger around it like pond-ripples until the whole thing (thought, pond, life, world) is a confused mass, all its molecules vibrating against each other.

Settling. Growing. Summer beginning to steam. It's becoming hard to ignore this baby-lump, the effort of moving it around. I start to envy Mum and Pug their lightness on their feet, their balance, their swiftness. My shoulders, neck, arms and legs seem to belong to a different body, one that hasn't been inflated like the middle of me. The strain of it is marking my belly skin with long red marks like scratch marks, that itch like crazy but are tender to touch. The books say these will fade in time, to silver—*fade* to silver?—but never absolutely disappear. I'm just worried I'll be stretched beyond endurance and split right open. Sometimes the whole lump goes drumskin-tight, when I first stand up, for example. That's why you see pregnant women always laying their hands on their lumps: to hold them in, to take a bit of the load off the stretched flesh.

By four weeks after the end of the birth classes, everyone in the class has had their baby except me, and I've three weeks to go. I'm literally holding up the party—they have a reunion when all the babies are born, a sort of show and tell. Fiona has called me a couple of times and given me a run-down on everyone else's births: how Linda was induced and had a short but howlingly painful labour; how Dean and Tracey nearly had theirs on the M4 and didn't make it to the birth centre; Angela's textbook twelve-hour water birth, and so on. Now there are six new healthy people in the world, six new families in various states of shock. It feels lonely being the only one left to go through it; I know there's nothing physically wrong with waiting, and that the baby will come when it's good and ready, but I'm getting tired of being occupied by this ferocious little animal with its shifting head and rib-kicking feet. I want my body back. I look at the clothes in my cupboard that I can't wear, and even the ones I wore when I was six months' pregnant look like they belong to a stick figure. Now I live in giant T-shirts and leggings. Now I'm officially that great blue woman from my first visit to the birth centre, invisible behind the evidence of my baby.

Pug and I spent this morning over at Justin and Nina's. And Paul's. Paul is the first child I've been allowed to get a good, close look at.

I don't know how Nina and Justin keep up with him. He never stops. For a while he sat quietly building a big tower with giant

155

Lego blocks, but then he was hungry and then he was thirsty and then he wanted to play in the sandpit and then he needed a nappy change and then he had to have a play with the hose and had to be changed again and then he wanted a biscuit, and on it went. He was like a very complicated pet. And this was a child you could *talk* to, who understood 'dangerous' and 'hot' and 'don't hit'.

'What was your life like when he was newborn?' I asked Nina.

She and Justin looked at each other and laughed. 'It was a bloody nightmare,' said Justin.

'It was. When he started sleeping through the night it got better, but for the first six weeks . . . we nearly went off our heads, didn't we, Justin?'

'Yeah. Then it was great for six months—take him anywhere, he'd sleep anywhere, he smiled at everyone. He was such a gorgeous kid. Then he got moving . . .'

'And he hasn't stopped since!' Nina gives a slightly hysterical laugh. 'Like, he's all right if you put him in the stroller, but you can't stop or browse in shops or anything or he starts wanting to get out, screaming and throwing himself around. He's a bit of a handful. But he still has a sleep in the afternoon, so we get a break then, and he's good at night—except when he's getting teeth, when he's terrible. So . . .' She looks at me and grins. 'We survive. We wouldn't know what to do with ourselves now, if we didn't have him.'

'Nope,' says Justin, fishing a pebble from Paul's mouth. 'He sure knows how to fill up the days.'

Paul's very sweet-looking, anyway, blond and smiley, with chunky little arms and legs. He's really firm about what he does and doesn't want to do, and quite friendly, not shy at all after the first few seconds.

One interesting thing I noticed: when Justin plays with Paul they become the centre of attention, everyone joining in or commenting. When Nina does anything with him they go off somewhere else, or sit to one side, and the 'grown-ups' talk that goes on doesn't include them unless Nina makes a point of contributing—which she does quite often, which makes me a bit less uncomfortable with the situation.

Nina seems much smarter than Justin. A couple of times she winks at me when he's raving on, but she never puts him down. They seem to work together well, as a couple, and as parents you can't say they're not dedicated. It's given me a lot to think about, that visit. I never thought before about the day-to-day-ness of having a child, the fitting in of things around sleep-times and meals and nappy changes. I try to think of Pug and me in Justin's and Nina's places, but I get distracted by the Paul figure, trying to see who that might be, that little girl- or boy-child, of *ours*, needing *us* to give it all those things, food and comfort and health and stimulation. The face—I need to see the face.

Mum and I have a talk about babysitting. It's not like she won't do *any*, but she reckons *one night a week* (and *not* Friday!) is all she's 'prepared to do'—and it always has to be the same night unless we make it another *by special arrangement*! And if I move out, *all* babysitting has to be done by special arrangement, and I have to bring the baby *to* her. I mean, she's got it all worked out even before she's *seen* the baby—I think that's the only way she can bring herself to be so cold about it. When it's born she'll be different—aren't grandparents always crazy about their grandchildren? Anyway, the whole thing makes me really *angry*, that she feels she has to get me to agree to this system, instead of just taking things day by day, seeing how they develop. And I have to sit there, 'Yes Mum, yes Mum,' with hardly any say in it at all.

'She's just trying to hang onto her own life, you know,' says Pug that night. 'She doesn't want to spend all her spare time at home looking after a baby, any more than you do.'

'Yeah, but somehow I thought she'd get more involved than she says she will. It's like she's pushing us all away from her, just when we had the chance to get close.'

'Oh, bullshit.'

'Stop laughing at me! What do you mean, bullshit?'

'How does dumping the baby on your mum and goin' off partying make you *close*?'

'It's not *that*. It's setting all these rules. It's like . . . I don't know, a boarding-house or something. Or *school*.'

'Oh, bullshit! Bullshit!'

'Stop *laughing*!' I turn away and lie on the very edge of the bed, stewing, embarrassed. He follows me, puts his arms around me even though I try to fling him off. 'Get away!'

He stops laughing. 'Hey. Hey. Mel. Ssh.' He holds me until I'm still. 'Listen. You listening?'

'Yes,' I say sulkily.

'Your mum's being so good about all this, we should both be down on our knees kissing her bloody feet, not hassling her to look after our kid. Christ, what are you worryin' about this for, now? Forget it. Look, she won't mind, if it's an emergency, if we're really goin' crazy, she won't mind bending those rules. It's just now, she's scared like you are, don't you reckon? 'Cause nobody knows what it's gunna be like with that baby being out here with us. And, shit, the lady's had enough stuff to cope with this year already, hey?'

'Did you know it's very sexist to call a woman a "lady"?'

'What?'

'You're supposed to call a woman (as opposed to a man) a woman, not a lady, as opposed to a *gentleman*. You're not supposed to put women on a pedestal like that.'

His grip relaxes. I turn back to find him gazing at me with an expression of immense patience, like a kindly grandpa. 'Like, am I just talkin' to myself here, mate? 'Cause if I am, you know, I'll just . . .'

'Oh, Dino, sometimes I really *enjoy* you.' I push my face in under his chin.

He sighs. His voice buzzes against my eyelids. 'Well, I don't know what the fuck you're on about half the time, but I enjoy you too. All right?'

'All right.' I surface and look at him, almost sick with happiness. 'Fine by me.'

He laughs through his nose. 'You are such a dickhead sometimes,' he says in his rustiest voice, the one where you can hear the squeak of the kid's voice through the rasp of the man's. 'Come down here, willya?'

'In Lucy,' Dr. Lovejoy said, 'notice that the birth process was somewhat more difficult. Her birth canal was broad but constricted from front to back. Her infant's cranium could pass through only if it was first turned sideways and then tilted.'
   Human birth is even more complex, according to Dr. Lovejoy. 'The much larger brain in the human infant demands a rounder birth canal. Even with the rounder birth canal, the human birth process is complex and traumatic, requiring a second rotation of the fetal cranium within the birth canal.'

I'm struck down by the flu. There's nothing like being eight and a half months pregnant *and* horribly sick—I honestly want to die. Worst flu I've ever had. It starts with feeling sick in the stomach and hurting all over, inside and out—feels as if even the *baby* is hurting! That goes on for twenty-four hours and then a horrible cold comes on, thick and poisonous so I can hardly breathe. I thought I felt stupid before, but now I spend my days slumped around the house with my mouth open to breathe, completely blobbed out. I'm cramming in vitamins but they make no difference *at all*. And I have to keep away from Pug because he's got a fight on Friday night. Another reason to be miserable.

The first time I see him in four days is when he comes down the aisle with Jimmy. I don't like the look of him—he just doesn't have his usual glow.

He fights badly, moves heavily, takes a lot of punishment. I'm nearly crying watching him coming back round after round. After the third round he's just defending himself, and sometimes not even very well. We have five rounds of Klaus Hupper getting

cockier and cockier, bulldozing Pug up against the ropes, opening the cut beside his eye again. This is at Kingsford, too.
Although there's a big bunch of Pug's supporters in the crowd,
most people are on Hupper's side. So they all think he's in ter-
rific form and Pug's just crumbling in the face of his skill, whereas
anyone who knows Pug can tell something's wrong with him.

In the end Hupper wins on points, though the win is so obvi-
ous that his fans start cheering as soon as the last bell goes.
Jimmy's there to catch Pug when his legs give way *two seconds*
after the bell. He holds him up, getting blood all over the shoulder of his shirt, until Pug comes to enough to be helped to his
corner. It's lovely to see those guys being so gentle and motherly
with him, towelling him down, making him have a drink.

When we get back to the change-room Pug smiles at me and
shakes his head. 'Feel shockin'. Even the bits that didn't get hit.'

'You done good, Dino, you done good,' says Jimmy, making
him sit down. 'Never touched the canvas once.'

'Felt like lyin' down and goin' to *sleep* on the bloody canvas!'
He sounds stuffed up, and there are big dark rings under his
eyes.

'I'm off my face,' he complains in the car on the way home.
We compare notes and figure out we must have the same bug.

I decide to stay over at Pug's place. He goes straight to bed
while I potter about. I have a shower. I put all the magazines in
a neat pile and all the socks and undies and dusty T-shirts in a
garbage bag for the laundromat. I've never tidied up a single
thing over at Pug's place before, but I find myself obeying some
kind of compulsion, unable to stop once I've started.

He's sprawled all over the bed and I don't want to wake him
up to move over, so for a while I sit and just look at him in the
combined moon- and streetlight. His face is a mess, as bad as it
can be without bones being broken—warped out of shape with
swellings around his mouth and right eye, where the blood teems,
repairing squelched cells, rinsing away the broken bits. I touch

his face and feel the heat of the work; he's too far down in sleep to react.

A little pain goes whispering under my belly, like lightning through a thundercloud. It's different from all other twinges and pressures of pregnancy. It's like the very edge of a period pain, nine months unfamiliar.

I sit listening, and five minutes later there's another one, and then (it seems like a miracle every time) every five minutes after that. *It's ready already.*

I make Pug move over, and I lie down, because all the books say you should try and get some sleep early on and save your energy, but of course I'm too excited and have to keep checking the contractions by my watch. They're so regular—I can tell myself, *You'll have another one in one minute*, and *exactly* sixty seconds later there's that little pain-whisper. It's really exciting being the only one awake and knowing. I lie there arguing with myself whether to wake Pug up—he's said he wants to know as soon as it starts, but he's sick and looks terrible and really would be better off sleeping. So I creep about, going to the toilet about fifty times, coming back to bed to count and doze and try not to panic.

Nothing more happens all night, just those regular, lightning-like pains. At about five, when the sky's getting light, one of them wakes me up, a proper cramp this time. I stare at the ceiling, alarmed, waiting for a catastrophically bad one, but the next few are weaker.

At six-thirty I touch Pug's shoulder. He opens his eyes, closes them again and says 'Y'okay? You've been up and down like a bloody yo-yo all night.'

'It's started.'

He opens his eyes (the right one only opens about halfway, it's so swollen) and stares at me. 'What, already? But you're not due!'

'They said any time two weeks before or two weeks after the due date.'

'Will it be okay?' He sits up.

'Beats me, but it's coming whether it's okay or not.'

He starts pulling on his clothes. 'Great, maybe they'll have a spare bed I can use in Intensive Care.'

'You look like a bomb blew up in your face.'

'That's how I feel, too. *You* look okay, but. How's your cold?'

'Not bothering me. I've got more important things to think about.'

We walk to Stanmore, and on the way I have to stop and think about a couple of these pains that hold on for longer and are quite crampy. Pug watches me closely, then when the pain stops he goes into an imitation of Fiona's assistant at the classes. 'What's she say? "Visualise." *Visualise* a flower opening, Mel—"slowly, slowly, all the petals. Helps your"—what's it called, where the head comes through?'

'The cervix.' I'm laughing.

'Yeah. Helps the cervix open. Go on, Mel, visualise a flower.'

'A *flower*. This is *muscle*! These muscles've been holding this baby up for eight and a half months! This is going to take some *work*.' I have a flash of fear then.

Pug can tell. 'We'll be at your Mum's soon.' He takes my hand.

The morning goes past in a flash—I can't believe it when Mum says, 'How about some lunch, then?' and it's twelve-thirty! By this stage I have to stop doing anything but breathing at the very top of each contraction, even though they're still exactly five minutes apart. 'I'm going to have to start making a noise soon,' I warn them. Mum rings the birth centre and we go through all the revolting business of getting there, which means three super-strength contractions (in five minutes) and my waters breaking all over the towels as I kneel on the car floor in the back, leaning on the back seat with Pug holding my hands and saying, 'Sounds just like Fiona said it would. You must be doing everything right.' I'm embarrassed at having yelled out and leaked everywhere, and so angry I could slap him, except that I'm too terrified of the next contraction. It's okay for *him*, it's happening *outside* his body.

When we get to the hospital they help me in. I'm *so glad* to

162

see Lois, the midwife—I feel like telling her to send Mum and Pug away! But once we get into the suite I just don't get the time. Lois does an internal examination, which brings on another pain, and tells us that I'm three centimetres dilated—a measly three centimetres after a night and half a day! I'm so pissed off and so scared of how much worse it might get!

All afternoon (it lasts forever, but it's over in a few seconds) the contractions go on, getting harder, stronger all the time. It's like a nightmare where I'm standing looking up a cliff face, knowing that a huge chunk of it is going to come loose and fall on top of me. Then I *see* it coming loose and all the rocks come thundering down and I feel them crushing me and burying me, but none of them just kindly knocks me out—I have to *feel* each one thudding into me. Then it eases off—but there I am again, at the bottom of the cliff, looking up and *knowing* that that rock-face is going to give way again.

I get into the rhythm of it. To save my body from screaming chaos, I have to. I'm kneeling beside the bed on some thin mats and I work out that I can *just* get through each one by hanging onto Pug's and Mum's hands as hard as I can and yelling 'A-a-a-a-ah!' on and on at the top of my voice—some of the pain disappears out my mouth then. Knowing that doesn't make me feel any better, though. I can't *believe* I got myself into this.

At about five o'clock everything stops dead. Lois tells me I'm fully dilated. I didn't even feel her examine me—in between roaring I'm half-asleep, stupid, and the far end of my body doesn't seem to belong to me any more. They have to lift me around to face the room in the squatting position I chose (like a gift from a catalogue) during the birth classes, way back when, in the life before I was in labour. 'You're all set now, Mel,' Lois says very clearly, as if to a deaf person. 'So if you feel like pushing, go right ahead.'

'God, who's got the energy to *push*?' I say, rolling my eyes at Pug.

'You have, mate. Somewhere in there. Don't worry. It'll come.'

And it does, the very next contraction, which is just *huge*. I can feel it coming a long way off ('Oh God, oh God,' I hear myself whimpering), and I get a good grip on Pug and Mum's arms. My throat closes off and I feel—little baby, I feel your head start to move down inside me. Before the contraction is even properly finished I have to tell them all, 'I felt the head moving!' All of a sudden I see the point of it all—it's as if I'd *forgotten* there was a baby right up until that moment. Now I'm incandescent with excitement—it's only a matter of *minutes* till we *see*, after all those months!

'Yes, we've got a head here.' Lois produces a mirror from nowhere and, God!, there you are: I'm gaping open a little to show a wrinkled piece of grey skin with dark streaks of wet hair on it. 'Fuck me dead!' whispers Pug, squeezing my hand very suddenly—I think he's going through the same realisation as me. Mum runs her hands through my wet hair, lifting it dripping off my neck. 'Nearly there, you *soldier*, you!'

Somehow during the next push I manage to keep my eyes on the mirror and I see your head ease out. It turns as it eases, and I can feel the turning inside me, the full stretch of myself making way for you.

'Look, it's got your eyebrows,' I joke hoarsely to Pug. What a cool customer I am, after all that roaring.

And here I am, half-delivered of a baby, as I've never been able to imagine I'd be. A face at both ends, like a Queen on a playing card. Your eyes are closed, your nose is blunt, your mouth all bunched up and cross-looking.

'Now just gently push the shoulders out, Mel, with the next contraction.'

Well, I do, but not just the shoulders come out. The whole baby slithers out in a rush, Lois neatly catching it and laying it on the padding between my feet.

'A girl!' says Pug, as if it was the last thing he'd expected to see!

I'm totally amazed, staring and staring. Her head was whitish grey, but as soon as she's out she starts flushing pink, all over, very quickly. She opens her mouth and there are gums in there, and a tongue as fine as a kitten's. Out of her throat on her first breath comes a tentative cry, a voice never heard in the world before. From her navel the live multicoloured umbilical rope spirals back up to my insides, to that beautifully positioned placenta.

'You could pick her up,' says Lois, and I do, astonished that I'm allowed to, that she's mine. She's so *hot* and damp and rubbery, but not slippery at all. Her arms shoot out and her fingers spread in surprise, even though I'm as gentle as I can be. She stops squeaking and opens her eyes—oh, *eyes*!

Pug is—everything is on his face that you and your new mother could hope for (except for the bruises). He looks wrecked, sick, unshaven—heaps worse for wear than I feel! His hands are fists at his mouth, and he's staring at you as if he's terrified you'll evaporate in front of his eyes. Tears run, ignored, down his face into the stubble.

'Come here,' I say, and he crawls over and sits with his head on my shoulder, gazing at you, touching your hair, your ears, your hands and feet, swearing in a shaky voice. All the time you frown at him in a really *outraged* way, but you don't make a fuss. Above me your grandmother blows her nose and says, 'Oh dear, oh dear, she's so lovely.'

You are such a marvellous little body, and somehow a personality, too, filling all the space in the room like a wind, making us all glow.

One last contraction approaches, nothing like as strong as the ones that brought you, and Lois is there with a metal dish to catch the placenta as it shlooshes out, wonderfully soft after your hard head. The umbilical cord is blanched-looking now, no longer beating.

'Here, Dino.' Lois hands him a pair of surgical scissors. Then she clamps off the cord near your belly and invites him to cut.

'Oh, God.' He sounds mildly hysterical, but he does it. And

there you are, with that enormous yellow toggle hanging off your tiny belly full of such complicated workings—including the workings for growing a baby, a tiny uterus like a pear tomato tucked away for future use. Have one, won't you? Whatever age, I don't mind. Because I want you to know what I feel, that the whole meaning of my life arrived in this birthing room, that I saw the point, seeing you, that I knew. I couldn't feel less like crying; I couldn't feel sturdier or happier or less embarrassed about my body than when they help me unfold it and lift it limb by limb onto the bed, puffy and saggy and bruised and leaking blood. Such good work it's done, such a prize it's delivered, just the way Mum said. What a system! Who worked this one out? Call them in here! I want to congratulate them!

She was born at 6.45 p.m. They let me stay in the birth centre overnight, which is great because Pug can stay too. The three of us sleep together on the double bed, the baby between us. In the middle of the night she starts wriggling in a slow, underwater kind of way and giving creaky little cries, so I sit up and give her her first breastfeed with the help of Joella, the midwife on duty. The baby falls back to sleep after a few minutes of feeding, but Pug and I are both wide awake by then, and we start talking. We go through all the names we'd been considering, but none of them seems right for this creature, the newness, the *ours*-ness of her. Then Pug, muttering to her in Italian, drops the word 'bella', and we decide that Bella is about as right as we'll ever get.

'What if she grows up really ugly, though?' I say.

'You're joking. Look at that skin.' Warm, pink, pearly. 'Look at that hair.' A fluff of black down. 'Check out those eyebrows.' The faintest curved black brushstrokes. 'You've gotta be joking.'

Then we get onto talking about the labour. 'It's . . . it's rough stuff,' he says, and I look at him and his eyes are filling up again. He puts his face in my shoulder and mutters, 'I thought it was never going to end. It was real easy to imagine . . . that . . . that she'd get stuck and you'd both die.' I feel a tear run down inside the neck of my T-shirt.

'Yeah, well, dying seemed like a pretty good option a couple of times there.' I'm trying to joke him out of it but I'm a bit wet-eyed myself. He takes a corner of Bella's cotton blanket and wipes my eyes and nose. 'Thanks.'

'That's okay.'

We both giggle. Then he kisses me with his bruised mouth, which is somehow really, really sexy—it has to stand in for the whole act of ⊕⊖, plus a few other things, new things, twenty-four hours' worth of things between us that can never be unmade, that can never, ever have not happened.

Sunday night and I'm home at Mum's on the hospital's early release programme. I've given Bella four feeds, and I'm starting to get used to that, even though she doesn't get proper milk for a day or so yet. Mostly she sleeps, recovering from the shock of arriving—and also that's when she grows, a nurse told us this morning. So sleep on, little baby, grow!

She's wrapped in a bunny rug in the Family Heirloom, parked behind my bedroom door. I'm supposed to be resting my poor bruised body while Pug and Mum organise dinner, but I struggle out of bed and sneak over for a private look at her, for the thrill of having her here to look at, instead of inside me, a total mystery. It's new every time I look at her; every time I find something else to notice. She must be growing so fast, so much going on inside that thin red skin, behind that sleeping face, those two loose fists the size of the ends of my thumbs. Unbelievably small and quiet. This little *person* who spent eight and a half months *inside me*. The ghost I saw kicking, just a few centimetres long, on the ultrasound screen, now an air-breathing person with a hardly-used voice, and a fresh-cut mouth hardly a centimetre wide, and grey-blue eyes (mostly crossed when they're open!). *You* were the one who made me sit up, jamming your feet under my ribs, who woke me with your stretching and squirming, who pushed your head up against my bladder fifteen times a night! It's lovely to meet you, *finally*.

God, this motherhood stuff, it does things to you! I walk out onto the front veranda in the afternoon, lightweight and unbalanced without my lump, without Bella in my arms.

Mum's sitting in one of the new cane chairs reading an interior decorating magazine. She looks up.

'She's asleep,' I say.

'Why aren't you, then?'

'I'm just seeing what it's like to be awake while she sleeps. Just for fun, you know.'

'Strange, I'll bet.'

'I don't know what to do with myself. Yes, I do—put on another load of washing.'

'You just sit tight there. She's going to wake up in three minutes, anyway.'

'Pug at training?'

'Yep. He's coming back afterwards, he says, so don't panic.'

'Good. I don't know how I'd've got through the last couple of nights without him.'

'Probably come and thrown Bella in with *me*! Thank you, Pug.'

'Thrown is right. That crying, I don't know, it really gets to me. I hear it and I can *feel* my heart speed up, and I just— aagh!—go so tense!'

'Yes, I remember that feeling with you.' Mum smiles. 'You just have to remember, it's not a personal attack on you, not an accusation that you're not a fit mother.'

'It sure sounds like it.'

'It's the only way she's got, to communicate. After a while you'll be able to tell which cries mean you have to get up and run to her, and which you can ignore.'

I grunt, reassured, irritated. So much to learn, *too* much. And we can't go about it systematically. Bella holds us to her own weird timetable, screaming demands (for *what*?), conking out mid-feed, sleeping for hours when we feel fresh and staying awake for hours when we're exhausted, pooing at all times of the day or night. We'll never get on top of this baby-care business, we'll never get it right.

'It does get better. Truly, it does,' says Mum.

I clutch the lifebelt of her sympathetic look. 'Well, I can't see how anyone'd ever get around to having second children if it stayed this bad.'

'Exactly, and they do. So hang in there. Try and relax. It's a period of adjustment.'

I stare across the road at the livid red bougainvillea snaking up the porch opposite. 'Why don't you just say: "Well, you brought it on yourself. You asked for it"?'

She laughs gently. 'I must be nicer than you think.'

Simone de Beauvoir: 'Babies filled me with horror. The sight of a mother with a child sucking the life from her breast, or women changing soiled diapers—it all filled me with disgust. I had no desire to be drained, to be the slave to such a creature.'

Gifts keep arriving. Almost every second day Pug turns up with something knitted or sewn or bought by one of his relatives. His mum is impossible—she can't go to the shops without finding something she *must get* for Bella, some ducks to string across her pram or a couple of singlets with roses embroidered on them, lacy bonnets, bibs, bunny rugs, miniature pillowslips. The woman next door, who I'd never met before, bought Bella a sleepsuit, and someone from Mum's work, who I remember coming to dinner *years* ago, sent a gift home with her. I mean, here I was wondering why birth is a covered-up, taboo subject, yet everyone, down to total strangers peering into the pram on the street, actually celebrates with you when you've brought a baby into the world. Everyone wants to welcome it. It's really . . . sweet, touching. It makes you see a part of people that never shows itself on any other occasion.

The strangest is the evening Dad turns up with a beautifully wrapped box, and holds it out to me as if he's really not sure whether I'll take it. Mum, Pug and I are out on the veranda taking turns holding a very awake, alert Bella.

'It's something Rick made,' says Dad. 'For the baby,' he adds, thrusting the box at me, almost pleading. *Bella doesn't hate us, yet, does she?*

'Ricky?' says Mum. '*Knitting?*' She manages to sound incredulous and neutral—you can *hear* her damping down the sarcasm.

'She sewed it.'

Mum's thinking, *Whatever for?*

It's one of those parcels it's a shame to unwrap. I take off the rosette and stick it on Bella's forehead while I unwrap the rest. Inside the box I push aside layers of cream tissue paper, to find a nightdress of soft cream cotton, with a collar, a pin-tucked yoke and three pearl buttons down the front. It's very simple, but about the classiest-looking garment Bella owns.

'Oh, that's lovely! Look, Mum, not a bow or a flower or a piece of lace anywhere.'

'It is nice,' Mum has to admit. Then she's biting her lips closed.

I don't know what to say—it's a lovely present, but if I'm too nice about it I'll be betraying Mum. I can't quite think what Ricky's trying to say here—is this her brown-nosing, or has she too been bitten by the baby-welcoming bug? I'm stuck there, the nightdress in my hand, not knowing whether I've actually accepted it, not knowing whether to laugh or shudder.

Pug comes to the rescue. 'You'll have to tell her thanks,' he says to Dad. 'Mel and me'll drop by one time with the baby and say hullo, hey Mel?'

'O-okay. I suppose.' I can't imagine it, though.

Here it is—she's nearly a week old and every day and night is like a whole lifetime—people coming and going, feeds, burps, nappy changes, cries, sleeps, baths—I look back and all I see is posset cloths and yellowed nappies and milk-stained T-shirts and pots of pawpaw cream and bottles of surgical spirit and cotton buds, and my huge clumsy hands wavering over Bella, learning to hold her steady in the bath and ignore her screaming for long enough to wash all her linty, sweaty, rash-spotted crevices.

The worst time so far has been when Pug was away at training and Mum hadn't got back from work, and Bella had this huge poo after having screamed for half an hour. I thought she was *dying* until I remembered to check her nappy and it was filling, filling with that yellow, sweetish-smelling froth that just goes on and on. I hung onto her while she screamed in my ear, put a tea-towel round her when the stuff started leaking down her legs (but not before it was all over my T-shirt—which was already pretty cheesy—and had blobbed on the loungeroom carpet). I cleaned her up in my room, discovered she had nappy rash, slathered her with cream—then the pooing continued. I stood there watching it go all over the freshly applied cream, all over the nappy, tears running down my face, *ridiculously* upset when you consider what a tiny thing it was, not exactly a disaster. While I cried and Bella pooed I changed my top, then when she'd finished (it was all over her feet as well, of course) I cleaned her up again, put on a fresh nappy and lifted her onto my shoulder, where she did a huge burp and sicked up milk all over herself, me, the floor and my bedspread.

I never thought I could feel even the tiniest bit angry with my own baby, let alone angrier than I've *ever* been in my life before! I felt like a madwoman, actually *shaking*, terrified I was going to throw her against the wall. I heard Mum's voice in my head, saying 'I did *warn* you!' and that made me even wilder—like, why didn't she make me *listen*, why didn't she tell me *properly* what this was going to be like?

Then I put Bella down really, really carefully on the change table. They say never leave them there, but I went to the bathroom and got a washer, came back, took off my T-shirt, washed myself, sponged the vomit off my shorts and shoes, off the carpet, off the bedspread. Bella was crying all the time, dark red all over, her arms and legs up in the air *vibrating*. It was like having screws drilled into my skull. When everything was cleaned up I went and got another washer, changed Bella's clothes and wiped her top half down (not as gently as I could have—I feel terrible when I think of it), put a clean suit on her and finally picked her up again when this gigantic rush of pity swept over me, cancelling out my anger and making *me* cry. At least she stopped crying when I picked her up. I tidied up all the mess one-handed, carrying her around, back and forth with cloths, out the back to the bin with the nappies, and then she was asleep, worn out with all the *trauma*, so I put her down in the Family Heirloom. Then I got out of there—went out and perched on the garden bench and read one of Mum's house magazines and pretended I was childless and fashion-conscious like all the people in the pictures, all the writers of the articles. It took me the whole magazine to stop shaking.

Pug comes out to help me with the pram—he and Mum probably heard Bella half-way down the block. 'I couldn't get a *word* in!' I'm complaining as we struggle up the stairs, and even I can hear the hysteria in my voice.

'Gave you a hard time, did she?' says Mum.

'I may as well not have gone. This stupid *cow* in the shop comes up and says "Is she a *difficult* baby, then?" as if she was some kind of object in a *specimen case*—I couldn't hear myself *think* in there! I didn't even get to buy what I went for! Just for no reason at all she started this up—' I wave at the pram, in which Bella's still screaming.

'Hungry?' says Mum, lifting out the Bella-bundle and shushing at it.

'I fed her *heaps*, just before we left, remember?'

'Wet? No. Dirty? No. *Couldn't* be cold, on a day like this.'

'It's nothing!' I say. 'It's just—she hates me, that's all. I got her out and rocked her for a while, but she wouldn't shut up and I couldn't concentrate, and everyone kept gawping, and smiling, so I thought, "Blow it, I'll just go home! I can't stand this."' Pug puts a tentative arm around my waist.

Mum jiggles Bella up and down, examining her bright red face, then holds her against her shoulder. 'Why don't you two go for a walk?' she says above the screaming. 'Get out of earshot for a while.'

'I don't want to go for a walk!' I shout. 'I want to know what's wrong with her!' I shake Pug's arm off.

'Probably nothing, sweetheart. Yelling won't help calm her down, though,' Mum says calmly.

I take Bella from her, roughly. '*Don't* you criticise me in front of her!'

Mum's empty hands stick out in front of her. Pug folds his arms and looks at the floor.

'She's *mine*!' I go on, my voice shaking. 'I *won't* let you take her over! You think now because we're here you *own* us, me, Bella, even *Dino*! You think you can organise everything the way *you* want, monopolise *everything*!'

'Mel, it's okay,' Mum says. 'Just calm down and Bella will calm down too.'

'Come on, it's not your mum's fault.' Pug puts his arms out for Bella. I shout past him. 'You think you know it all! Well, I'm a mother, too, and I have instincts, too, and this is *my* daughter and *I* know what's best for her.'

Mum's arms drop and her stunned look gives way to something more decisive. 'All right. Fine. If you know what's best.' The words are barely audible. She pushes between me and Pug and goes out onto the front veranda. Bella's wailing goes on and on in the silence.

I don't look at Pug. I'm hanging on to Bella just a little too tightly. 'Shut up, shut up, shut *up*,' I hear myself saying. I'm shocked at how nasty I sound.

Pug takes hold of Bella. 'Give us her,' he says. I try to pull away. 'Come on, Mel, don't be a dickhead. Give us her before you hurt her.'

'No!' I growl, trying to step back.

'Come on! She's just a little baby.'

'She's just a little—fucking—*monster*!' I go to pieces. I hand her over. 'She screams at me, she won't let me sleep, she's sucking me to pieces. She's—always here! I'm sick of her! I'm sick of the sight of her! I'm sick of the *sound* of her, and I'm stuck with her for eighteen more years!' I end up nearly screaming.

'She won't be a baby all that time,' Pug says, far too reasonably.

'It's all right for you. You can come and go whenever you want. Even if you *don't* go,' I say as he gapes at me, 'you've got the *choice*. *I* haven't got the choice. I haven't got *any* choice—I'm just stuck here *serving* her, feeding, changing, bathing, having a heart attack every time she *twitches*—'

I slam out into the backyard, knowing the bang of the back door will frighten Bella, hoping savagely that it scares her into silence, hoping it scares her to *death*. I sit on the old garden bench by the Hill's Hoist, listening to Bella screaming on, the noise moving away through the house. *That's right—go and suck up to Mum.*

Eventually I'm able to hear birds, breeze. Insects zoom and tick in the grass. I stop shaking and hating them all, and turn to crying and hating myself. I'm not finished even twenty minutes later when Pug brings a glass of iced water out to me. He sits with me as I sip and sniff.

'I don't know how you can stand me sometimes,' I get around to saying.

'I can't, but if I want to see Bella I've got to keep things sweet with you, haven't I?'

Fresh tears roll out, when I'd just got them under control. 'Don't laugh at me!'

'I'm not!' He laughs. 'I'm trying to make you feel better, stupid.' He puts his arms around me while I sob on. I'll *never* be able to stop.

'She's gone to sleep, anyway, that monster,' he says. 'Your mum's got her.'

'So is Mum going to throw me out for being so rude?'

'No, I think you're gunna have to put up with her a while longer.'

'Oh God, I wish she wasn't so bloody *perfect*!' I sob. 'I always feel like I'm just slobbing around stuffing things up, and then she comes in and *fixes* everything, and *understands*!'

'It's a bad time,' says Pug. 'Who could think straight on four hours sleep a night? You're doin' okay. Everybody falls apart getting used to having a kid around.'

'You don't.' I look up at him accusingly.

He makes a doubtful face. 'Well, all I can say is, I'm glad my next fight isn't till January. I wouldn't last thirty seconds the way I am now.'

'You seem steady as a rock to me.'

'I dunno.' He takes his arms away, sits the way he does at the gym, elbows on knees, one knee and shoulder pressed against mine. 'You start thinkin' about all sorts of shit you never thought about before—like schools and shit, you know? And, God!, *wars*, and bloody *rainforests* and all that *conservation* bullshit that used to make me just wanna chuck. Do you do that?' he asks me.

'It's the future. It's having someone to pass things on to. *Heirs*. Long-term responsibilities,' I say glumly.

'Well, it's just about sending me nuts, all this thinking. I mean, really *heavy* stuff. Like *everything's* different.'

I nod. 'Everything. Sometimes I feel like the person I was has just puffed out like a candle. All that's left is a mess of wanting-to-do-the-right-thing and being-scared-for-Bella. I look at her and I'm just *petrified*, about all those things you say, about *everything*, about touching her, even. And I want to give up. It's too much for me. But I'm not allowed.'

'Yes, you are. Of course you are. But would you, I mean *seriously*? Think of someone else taking her on?'

'Absolutely! Yes. And then, next second, absolutely no. I mean, I get so exhausted, going *so far* down one minute, and so, *so* high the next. It's so violent and extreme—it's hopeless. It's probably hormones, but what's the difference? Biological misery *feels* the same as "real" misery, hey.'

He studies the matted kikuyu grass between his feet. 'I get it the same, but, and I don't have any of that stuff going on in my body. I sometimes think, "Shit, this was a *bad* mistake we made here." But then, you look at her, you pick her up . . . like, how can anything be so *little*, and still be *human*?! And then, when you think she'll be talking back to us in a couple of years, walking around, you know, like Paul, playing—' He grabs his head as if to prevent it exploding. 'I just reckon, if we can stick it out, this first bit, you know? There's just so much gunna happen, that's gunna be so cool. Don't you think? I mean, *think* about it!'

I already am, smiling. He looks at me. 'The first six weeks are the worst. That's what your mum says.'

'And she knows *everything*, of course.' I nudge his arm.

'So, you know, this is the worst it gets. After this things'll settle a bit and we won't know why we kept losin' it every ten seconds.'

'You'd better be right.'

'And tomorrow, when we go to that reunion, if Bel chucks a wobbly, just give her to me and I'll take her off somewhere where you can't hear, okay? Round the block a few times, or something. You got that?'

I nod. 'Thanks. Not just for that. Thanks for just sticking around, especially when I'm acting disgustingly.'

'Give yourself a break.' He kisses my cheek.

'What—arm, leg or neck?'

'I mean it. Go easy. You don't help no-one puttin' yourself down all the time. Come round the front and be nice to your mum; that'll make you feel better. You don't have to say sorry—' I resist him pulling me to my feet. 'Just sit with her and be nice, you know?'

'Oh, okay,' I say ungraciously and follow him around the house.

I wake up at about eleven in the morning. I lie in bed trying to piece together the last twelve hours. How many feeds did Bella have? She's due for one now, I can tell—my left breast is hard as a rock, hot with milk. Even as I notice it it starts to leak. Why isn't she screaming? I've grown so used to being woken up by her crying that it's weird to wake in a silent house. Weird, but *very* nice.

I try to add up the hours of sleep I got. I think it's about seven, but broken every hour, and I remember being awake from one to two and also for the dawn. That's okay, a total of seven means I'll be able to think about something other than sleep for the rest of the day. I remember handing Bella to Pug as he came in from morning training and veering into the bedroom and collapsing here. Now the room is a hot-box, the garden shrilling with cicadas.

I get up to change breastpads, pick up the last few days' milky, dribble-stained clothes, both Bella's and mine. On the way through to the laundry I pass Pug asleep on the couch, with Bella on his chest, also sleeping. I finish setting my room in order, sorting a load of Bella-clothes onto the shelves, making the bed, which I haven't had time to do for days. Then I go into the loungeroom and squat next to the couch, intending to wake Bella for a feed.

Then I think, *Why?* Obviously she's not hungry enough to be uncomfortable. Why hop back on the treadmill before you have to? They're both completely zonked, motionless except for Bella rising and falling with Pug's breathing. She's wearing just a nappy, and Pug's hand is on it, holding her steady. When they get up she's going to leave a wet print of her thin, froggy body on his T-shirt.

Pug's snoring delicate snores like a cat's, a single sticking in the throat on each breath. Bella makes no sound; I have to look really closely to differentiate her breathing from Pug's. She has such a different face, asleep, without those great dark eyes dominating. I hardly ever see it, these days, trying to get some sleep myself whenever she lets me. There's something foetal about it; she's filled out a bit, but she still has a pointed chin. Her skin's cleared up since a spotty few days after she was born; she looks almost as dew-fresh as in her first hours.

Mine. Both of these bodies and the people inside them. This time last year I'd only just met Pug, and now there's not only him, here in my home, but *her*, little *her*, whoever she's going to be. I can't believe her, can't believe I grew her and gave birth to her. I think over her birth almost every day. Sometimes I'm in despair, thinking, *I had no idea what I was starting, I just had* no *idea.* Sometimes I'm trying to catch back that certainty I had then, that absolute, wholehearted willingness to scale mountains, swim seas and fight off hordes of ravenous beasts if Bella's welfare required it, that strength I got from seeing how strong my body was, the extent of what it could do. I didn't think I would ever return from that to being my own old self, griping and getting bogged down in tiny day-to-day details. I thought, *Oh, at last I'm grown up, at last I'm mature and noble.* And I was. And if I could have frozen myself in the hours I spent in the birthing-room I would have stayed that way.

But I came home, and discovered here how *many more* tiny day-to-day details there are in a baby's life. And what details—the lowest of the low, bathing and bum-wiping, mopping up spew! Trying to put together a sentence, battling not to cry and scream yourself. Only just holding back from being an *animal*, let alone managing maturity, nobility! *I had no idea.* Everybody says, beforehand, 'Oh, you'll have your work cut out for you when the baby comes,' but you don't realise why they laugh that boy-I-only-just-got-out-alive laugh when they say it until you're caught in the same trap, climbing the same walls, discovering hour after hour how *im*mature and *ig*noble you can be.

It's only times like this—I back away from the sleepers and curl up in an armchair—times when you get a fragment of a break, that you can appreciate what's going on. You wonder what happened to that old, before-baby life, and what you were so het up about. God, all those people I hated—who'd waste time on them? (Time, which I had lashings of, then, which I have only the tiniest scraps of, now!) I used to care *so much* what Lisa Wilkinson thought—I remember, I used to try and dress in her style, even, for a while, which was when I first became visible to Brenner. And Brenner! What made me think we ever had *anything* in common? What made me think he ever cared two hoots about me? The more I think about it, the more I think the problem was that Brenner was just plain *boring*—he was just a superfit body kind of going through the motions of being alive. We never properly talked, just as Lisa and I never did—we always chattered on and cracked a lot of jokes, but nothing important ever got said. Talking with Pug, his words may come out all cockeyed and chewed apart, but he's always saying something—he doesn't just talk to make an impression. He's secure in himself that way.

All I can do now is feel sorry for those people. Looking at Bella, thinking about Jasper and Donna and Lisa, they're losing out so much (not that they'd think so!) by *not* sitting here seeing this baby, *having* her, having placed her in the world. They seem such tiny undeveloped creatures themselves, *playing* at being people, and getting it wrong. I got it wrong, too, really embarrassingly wrong, but now I'm starting to feel like a *human person*, which means looking out past your own *clothing* and what your body's telling you and your own feelings, and beginning to see everyone else. And, God!, everyone else used to be like Bella— they all lay, even boneheaded Brenner, curled up asleep, so soft and small and easily damaged that your heart just, oh!, fists tight with fear for them. *Someone* stared at them and wondered, utterly unable to imagine, what they'd be like at one year, at five years, at seventeen! *Someone* held them to be sacred, *someone's* life would have been ruined if they'd died.

And maybe, bringing them up, someone forgot, because of the details, the multiple and multiplying distractions, how miraculous they were, forgot about the full-blown person arriving and claiming breath, about the complete unconscious trust those little waxy red people had, from their first breath on. And they were allowed to go sour, somehow, and turn around and claw at the people who'd welcomed them, and anyone else within reach, i.e. me, i.e. everyone who wasn't a member of their group.

Forgetting—it's easy to do, when you're exhausted, and busy, when your child's been yelling all night, when you haven't got the time or energy to go to the toilet, let alone shower! Who could blame *anyone* for forgetting?

But there's nothing in place anywhere to make people remember. Pug's mum crosses herself every time she passes a church. If there were something like the crosses, the carvings, the stained-glass windows, the architecture of churches in maternity hospitals, in schools, in clinics, instead of them looking like barracks or prisons; if there were something to mark them as places where, every hour of every day and night, new people were arriving; if everyone noticed them and knew what they were about; if everyone believed, and crossed themselves, or slowed their cars, or took off their shoes, or laid their hands on their hearts, or *something*; if there was some ritual that included these places, these people in everyone's lives, whether they were parents themselves or childless, young or old . . .

But there isn't. There's only the people themselves, the pink, froggy babies sleeping away the hot morning, the fathers providing the body-noise that soothes them, the mothers sitting to one side with their breastpads sodden and the sweet scent of their own milk in their nostrils. There are only the families. And sometimes families stay families, and sometimes they stop being sacred or special, and disperse. And sometimes they form new families and sometimes they strike out on their own, but they always take something with them—some imprint, some way of seeing, feeling, acting or reacting, so that some ancestor walking out of the fifteenth century might recognise my shrug, or my hairline, or the way I laugh or lose my temper, as her own way, or her father's way; so that Bella lying on her deathbed with her great-grandchildren around her will hear them use my voice, or see her own face, or see Dad's scowl on one of them.

They didn't tell us this at school; they told us we were all

180

individuals carving out places for ourselves. No one ever warned me that someone else could take my heart and bare it to the world for breaking over and over again, the way Bella does. What did I think she was—some kind of *fashion accessory*, like a hand-bag, a poodle on a leash? Instead she's my *self*, morphed with someone else's so I can't see the joins.

Bella starts her hunger-howl even before her eyes open, desperate in an instant. The room is almost foggy with the smell of milk. I gather her up from Pug's chest, sit down, attach her to me. She glugs and chokes and shrieks. Then there's the mind-bend of the milk letting down, as if it's being pulled from my fingertips, from my tongue, from the roots of my hair.

In slow motion Pug sits up, yawns, rubs his face. Outside the cicadas cease, like a blanket snatched off us, letting cool silence in. Across the dimness, the milk-fog, the gulp and suck of Bella, the sheer impossibility of it all being real, I smile at Pug, and he at me. I smile and say, 'Good morning.'